BRAIN GAMES
kids

Mazes

pil

Publications International, Ltd.

Puzzle Constructors: Keith Burns, Myles Callum, Don Cook, Adrian Fisher, David Helton, Robin Humer, Steve Karp, Planet X Graphics, Pete Sarjeant, Andy Scordellis, Alex Willmore

Illustrators: Robin Humer, Shavan R. Spears, Jen Torche

Cover Puzzles: David Helton, Planet X Graphics
Cover Illustrations: Shutterstock

ISBN-13: 978-1-4508-1617-5
ISBN-10: 1-4508-1617-7

Manufactured in China.

8 7 6 5 4 3 2 1

CONTENTS

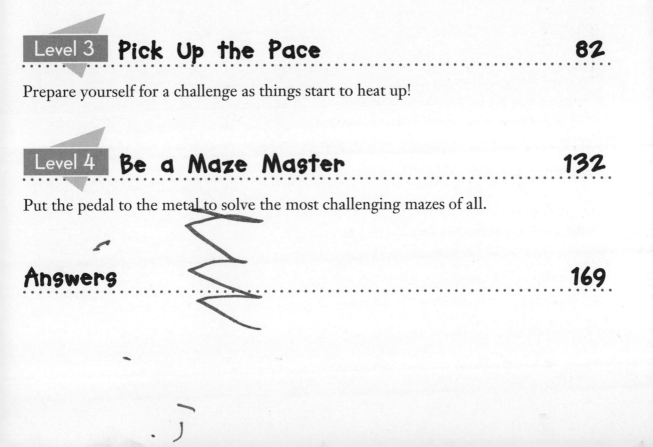

ALL PATHS LEAD TO FUN!

Hey, kids! Are you ready to have an a*maze*ingly good time—and challenge your brain at the same time?

Brain Games™ Kids: Mazes offers a huge collection of seriously cool mazes designed to give your brain a boost. Navigate a labyrinth of twists and turns to lead a pirate to his treasure, help a fish escape an octopus, take a spin on a wild waterslide, and so much more! *Brain Games™ Kids: Mazes* also features:

• Puzzles that have been sorted into 4 levels, which means you'll find the easiest puzzles at the beginning of the book. If you're really looking for a challenge, head straight to Level 4—those mazes are the trickiest.

• Answers to every puzzle at the back of the book. Just be sure to give each maze a fair try before peeking at the answers. You want to give your brain a full workout before throwing in the towel.

• Loads and loads of fun! No matter what maze you're tackling—whether you solve it in a snap or get hung up on it for what seems like ages—the most important thing to remember is to have fun!

Every day is a great day for puzzles, so open up to a maze right now!

Hello, parents! The pages of *Brain Games™ Kids: Mazes* are jammed with an exciting collection of mazes that will not only work kids' brains but will also provide them with hours of entertainment. They'll improve their planning and visual skills without even realizing it.

We've grouped the puzzles by difficulty level so you can help guide your child to the puzzles that will suit him or her best. Beginners will love working on the mazes in Level 1. Intermediates will feel right at home in the middle sections (Levels 2 and 3), while advanced puzzlers will love the mental challenge provided by the Level 4 labyrinths. The answers are included at the end of the book, so if they get stuck (or if you do!), just take a peek at the solution to get back on track.

Many educators agree that puzzles are among the best ways to engage children in the thinking process. Your mission is to get them started on the journey toward learning. So give them this book and turn them loose on puzzling!

GET MOVING WITH MAZES!

Dino-Mite Maze

Here's a safe way to have fun with a dinosaur! Enter at the right foot and scoot out at the tail.

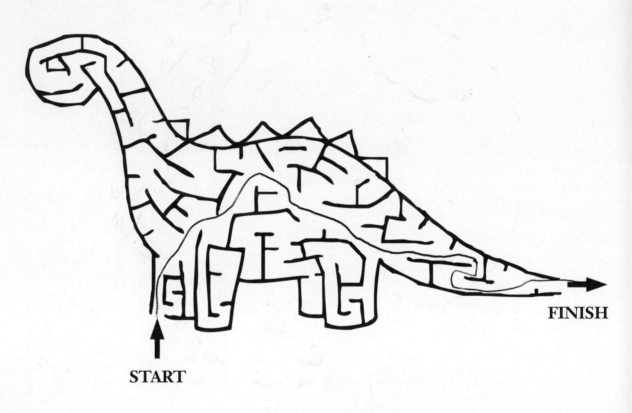

FINISH

START

Answer on page 169.

Tangled Triangles

Can you find your way through the tangled maze?

START

FINISH

Answer on page 169.

7

Alley Cat

Looks like lunch has arrived for this lucky cat. Get him to the free fish before another cat arrives.

Answer on page 169.

8

X Marks the Spot!

Ahoy, matey! This is a maze with a twist. Instead of searching for a clear path to the finish, find the solid black line that leads to the buried treasure.

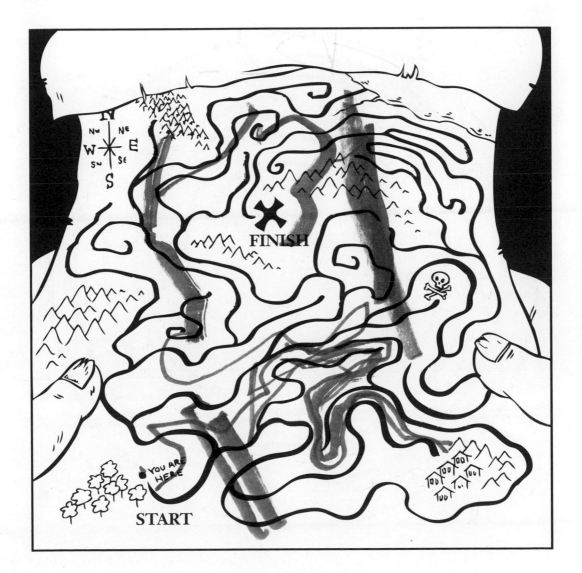

Answer on page 169.

9

Lost in Space

The astronaut wants to go home! Guide her through the maze and back to her spaceship.

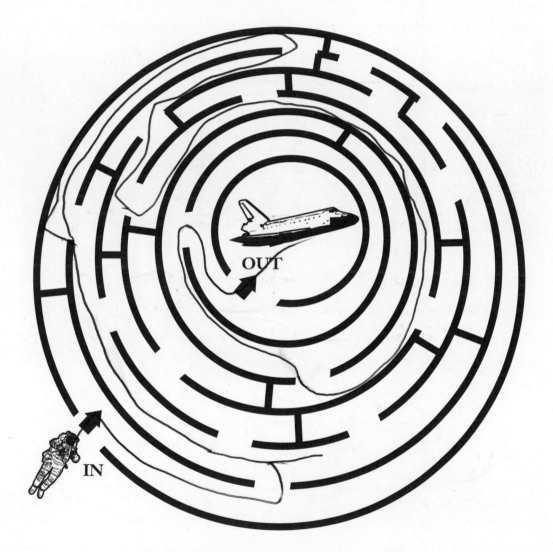

Answer on page 169.

Timer Maze

Get a watch or timer and see how fast you can make it through this maze. Can you do it in under a minute? How many seconds?

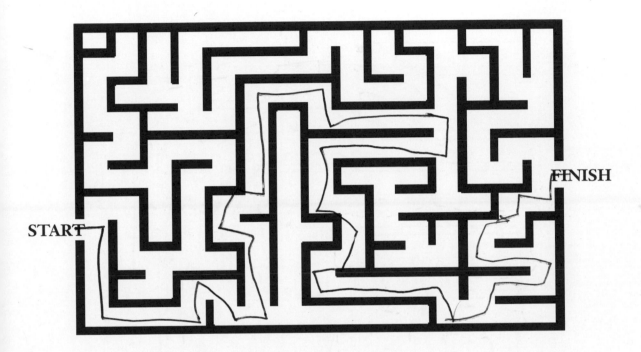

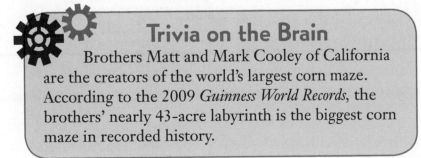

Trivia on the Brain

Brothers Matt and Mark Cooley of California are the creators of the world's largest corn maze. According to the 2009 *Guinness World Records*, the brothers' nearly 43-acre labyrinth is the biggest corn maze in recorded history.

Answer on page 169.

11

Hoops

Make the winning basket to be MVP of the game.

Answer on page 170.

Monster Mash

The mummy needs to get to the party, but first he needs to pick up some snacks. Lead the way!

Answer on page 170.

13

Feeling Antsy?

These hungry ants have set their sights on your birthday cake!

Trivia on the Brain

Most people would hate for ants to invade their picnic, but what if those ants were the main dish? Ants are on the menu in countries like Mexico, India, and Thailand and are often considered a delicacy!

Answer on page 170.

Box Maze

Can you guess why this box is smiling? Maybe he's thinking...outside the box?

START

FINISH

Answer on page 170.

Flower Power

Guide the butterfly to the flower at the end of the maze.

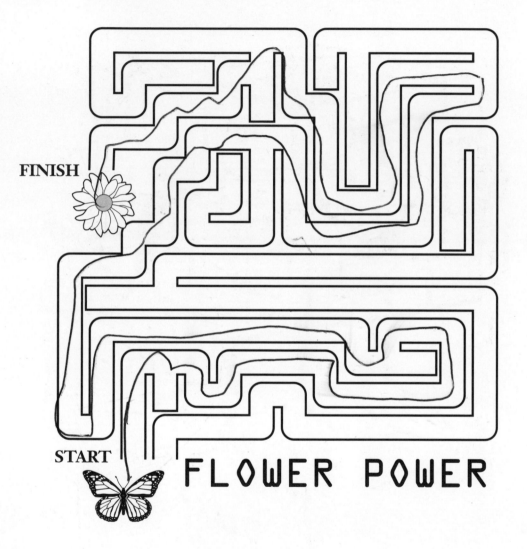

FINISH

START

FLOWER POWER

Answer on page 170.

Gone Fishin'

Grab your tackle box and get to the other side of the riverbank.

Answer on page 170.

17

What's Cookin'?

If you enter at the left handle, can you get out of the stew and exit the pot on the other side?

START   FINISH

Trivia on the Brain

The world's largest pot of baked beans was made in Pinson, Alabama, in September 2010. The 1,010.65 gallons of butterbeans were the centerpiece of the fifth annual Alabama Butterbean Festival.

Answer on page 171.

Swing Batter!

Follow the slugger's blast to the ball's location in the center of the maze.

Answer on page 171.

Bee Maze

Help the bee find its way to the flower at the center of the maze.

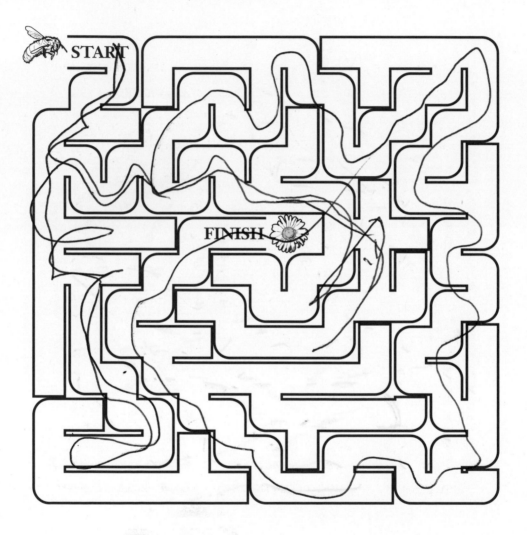

Answer on page 171.

Scrambled Squares

Can you find your way through the tangled maze?

START

FINISH

Answer on page 171.

21

Leapfrog

Grow from a tadpole to a hopping frog over the course of this maze.

Answer on page 171.

It's the Great Pumpkin Maze!

Before you start carving this Halloween pumpkin, take a quick tour through the inside.

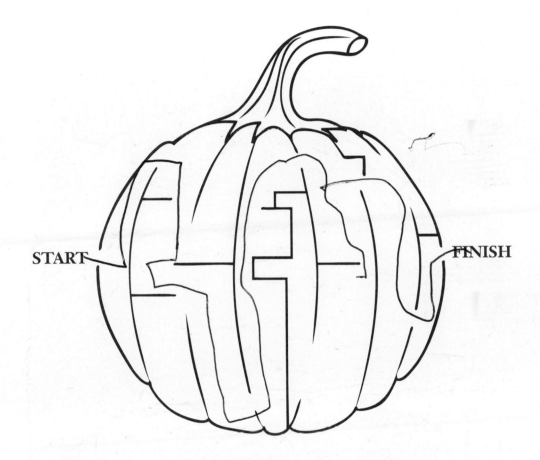

START   FINISH

Trivia on the Brain

The name "jack-o'-lantern" comes from Irish folklore. Originally, faces and pictures were carved into turnips, but when the Irish moved to America, they found that pumpkins made much better jack-o'-lanterns so they used them instead.

Answer on page 171.

Garden Path

Grab your seeds and wheelbarrow and head to the shed—maybe plant a few flowers along the way!

Answer on page 171.

24

So You Want to Be a Star?

Why is this guy smiling? Because he's a star! You'll be a star too once you complete this maze!

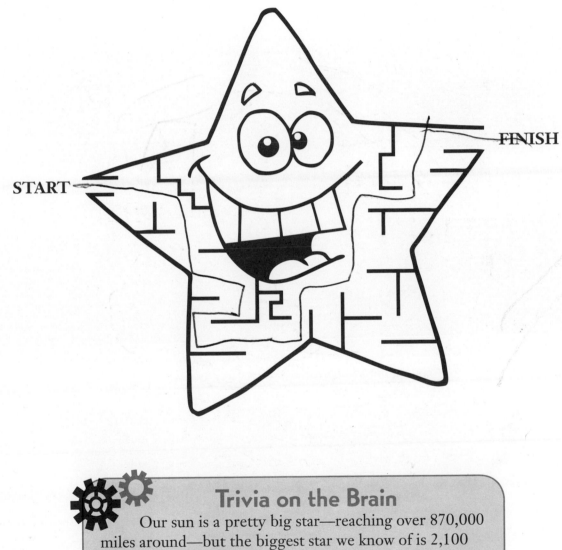

Trivia on the Brain

Our sun is a pretty big star—reaching over 870,000 miles around—but the biggest star we know of is 2,100 times the size of the sun. In comparison, the sun would be little more than a speck.

Answer on page 172.

Pizza Pie

Get that pizza in the oven as quick as you can!

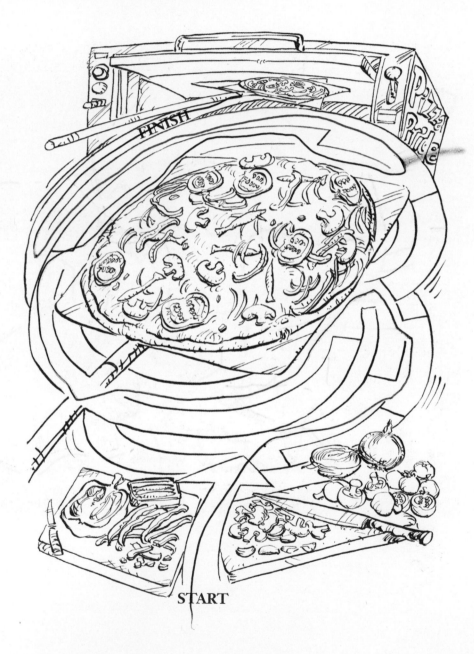

Answer on page 172.

Twist and Shout

Can you find your way through the tangled maze?

Answer on page 172.

Tentacles!

It's trouble in the sea! Help the little fish escape the octopus.

Answer on page 172.

28

David and Goliath

Before David can battle Goliath, he must first overcome this maze.

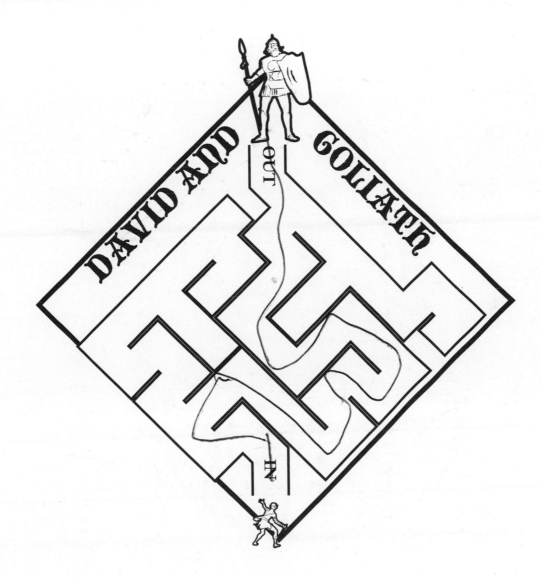

Answer on page 172.

Frosty the Snow-Maze

Can you make it through Frosty before he melts?

START

FINISH

Answer on page 172.

Dizzy Maze

This maze was supposed to have straight walls, but the maze builder was feeling a little dizzy that day, and this is what happened!

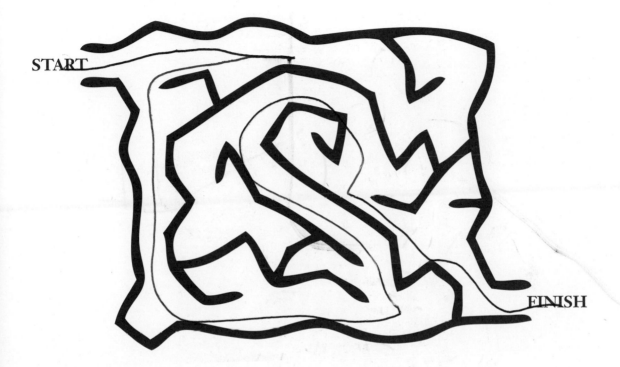

START

FINISH

Trivia on the Brain

Dizziness isn't really caused by the blurring we see when we spin around too fast; it has to do with the ear. Liquid in the ear canal sloshes around when we spin and that sends confusing messages to the brain. The dizzy feeling is your brain telling your body that the spinning has to stop!

Answer on page 172.

Get It Straight

Don't get too caught up in all the twists and turns as you negotiate your way to the center of this intricate wizard labyrinth.

Answer on page 173.

Knotted Network

Can you find your way through the tangled maze?

Answer on page 173.

Cottage Stroll

Walk along the country path to the open gates.

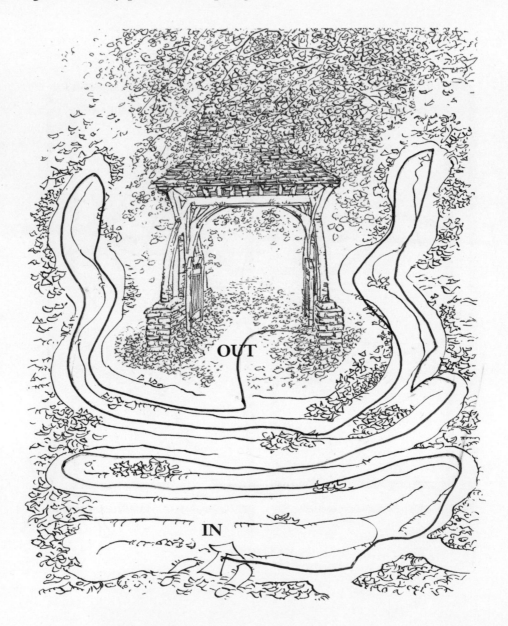

OUT

IN

Answer on page 173.

Home Run!

Follow the slugger's blast to the ball in the center of the maze and then out of the park.

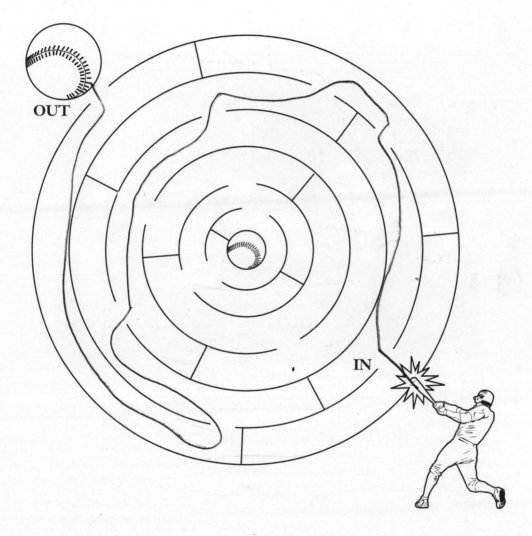

OUT

IN

Answer on page 173.

Pizza Delivery!

Deliver pizza in style—find the fastest route.

Answer on page 173.

Nell

Help Nell find her way through the maze.

FINISH

START

Trivia on the Brain

It isn't likely that Nell would lose her way home in real life because the old saying "an elephant never forgets" is close to the truth. Elephants have the biggest brain of all land animals, which helps them remember better and for much longer than almost any other animal we know of.

Answer on page 173.

Cat and Mice

Who will win this game of cat and mouse?

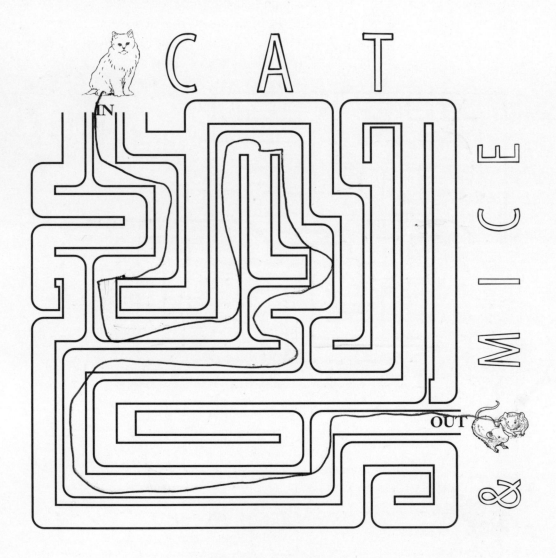

Answer on page 174.

A–Maze–ing Walk in the Park

It was a beautiful sunny day, so Jenny (J) took her new puppy, Sparky (S), for a stroll in the park. As they were starting out, Jenny bent down to tie her sneakers. When she let go of the leash, Sparky took off on a little romp of his own. Fortunately, a nice woman saw Sparky and picked up his leash, and they waited for Jenny at the exit. Can you get from J to S? You can travel over and under bridges if you need to.

Answer on page 174.

Honey Bear

Help the bear find a sweet reward at the end of the maze.

Answer on page 174.

Robot Recharge

Rodney needs a battery charge, but he'll have to go through the maze first.

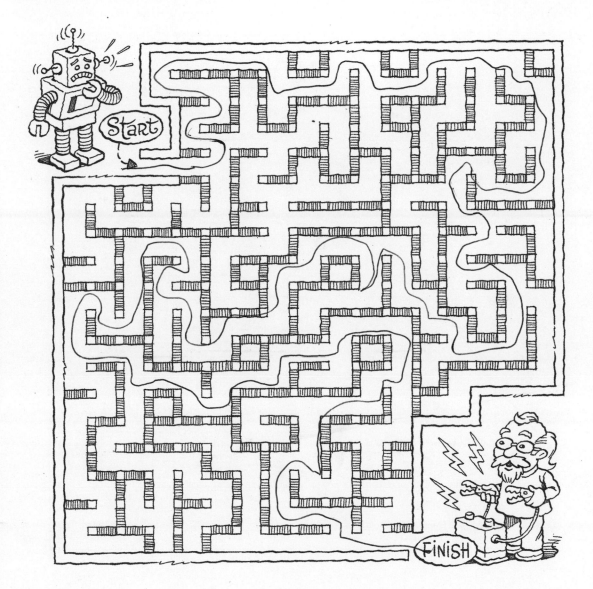

Answer on page 174.

41

Kittens

These cute kittens unraveled a ball of yarn. Start at the top of the maze and work back to the yarn ball.

START

FINISH

Answer on page 174.

Granny Smith

The road is blocked by sheep, and the delivery driver can't get through to Granny Smith. Can you help guide him over the dirt track?

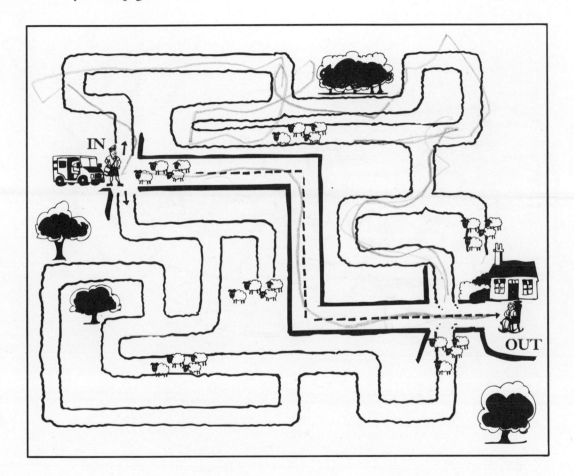

Answer on page 174.

43

A Whale of a Maze

If you enter at the whale's mouth, can you find your way out through its blowhole at the top?

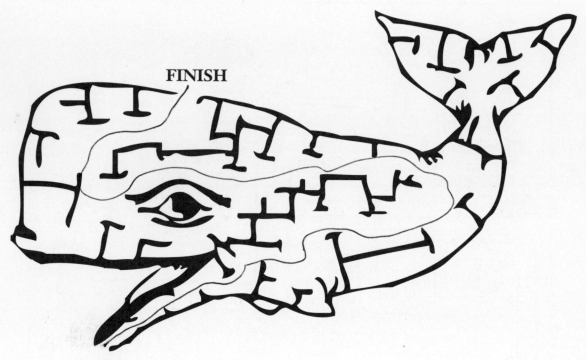

FINISH

START

Answer on page 175.

Alien Invasion!

The alien wants you to take him to your leader. Can you guide him through the crop circle maze?

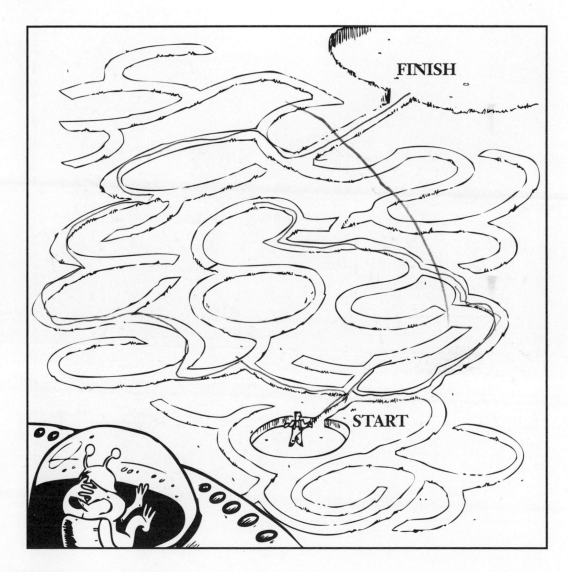

Answer on page 175.

Crumbs

Can you help the mice get to the food stuck in the wizard's beard?

Answer on page 175.

46

Nuts and Bolts

Help the robot reach its missing parts!

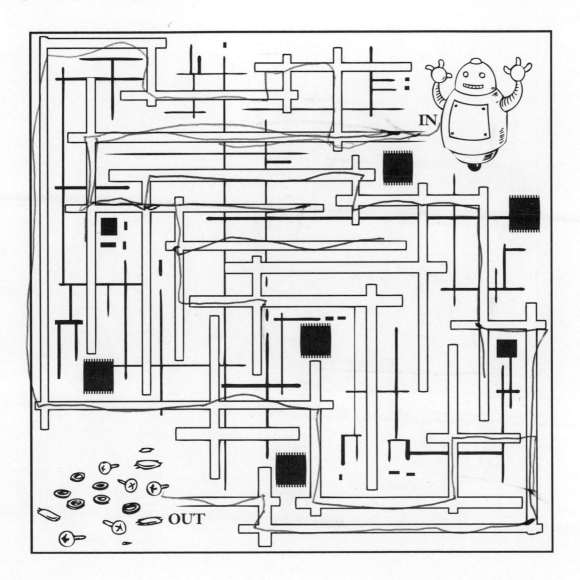

Answer on page 175

Caveman

Get the caveman safely home. Be sure to watch out for the dinosaurs!

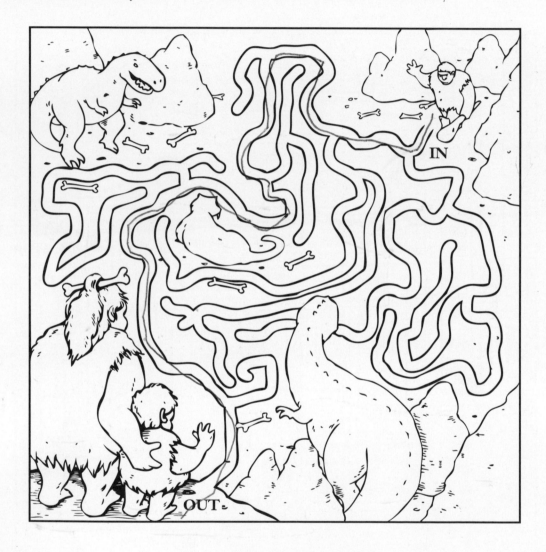

Answer on page 175.

Here, Fishy Fishy!

Swim your way around these fishy friends—just don't be mistaken for fish food!

Answer on page 175.

49

FIND A WAY THROUGH

Busy Bees

This bee wants to spend time with his friends. Help him get to their *hiveout*!

Answer on page 175.

Pondemonium

Timothy Turtle would really like to take a swim, but the pond is extra busy today. Help him reach the deeper part that's not so crowded.

Answer on page 176.

Yer Out!

Guide the path of the ball to the fielder's mitt.

Answer on page 176.

Warp Drive!

Take a journey through time and space as you complete this maze!

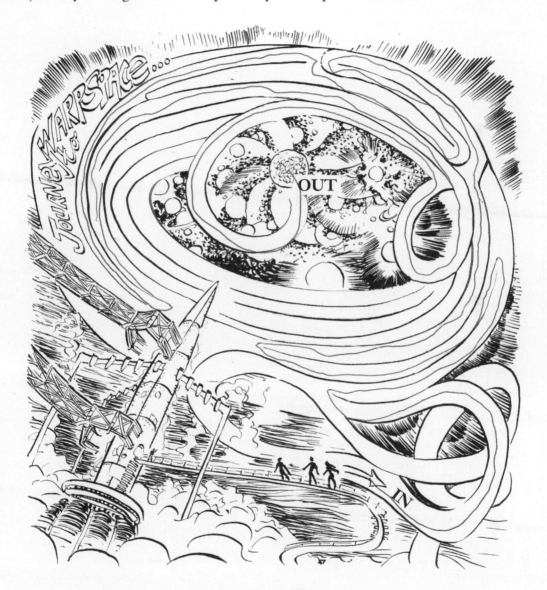

Answer on page 176.

Snack Attack

The man with the snacks in the upper-right corner needs a little assistance avoiding obstacles so he can get back to his seat in the bleachers and enjoy the game. Can you help him?

Answer on page 176.

Here kitty!

Choose the path that will get Possum home for dinner.

Answer on page 176.

Cafeteria Confusion

Jill wants to have lunch with John, but first she must find her way through the maze.

Answer on page 176.

Trapped!

Can you find your way through the tangled maze?

START

FINISH

Answer on page 177.

Garden

Can you help Haley find her way through the garden to have tea with her grandmother?

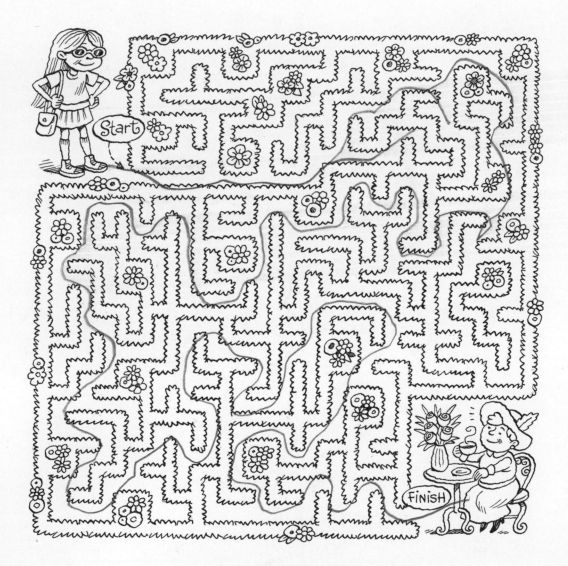

Answer on page 177.

Game Time!

Zap your way through the twists and turns of this maze.

Answer on page 177.

Wild Wally's Waterpark

Jump on an inner tube, and slide through the maze to the tropical lagoon below.

Answer on page 177.

Out of this World!

Guide the astronaut through the maze and back to his spaceship

IN

OUT

Answer on page 177.

Batter Up!

Follow the slugger's blast to the ball's location.

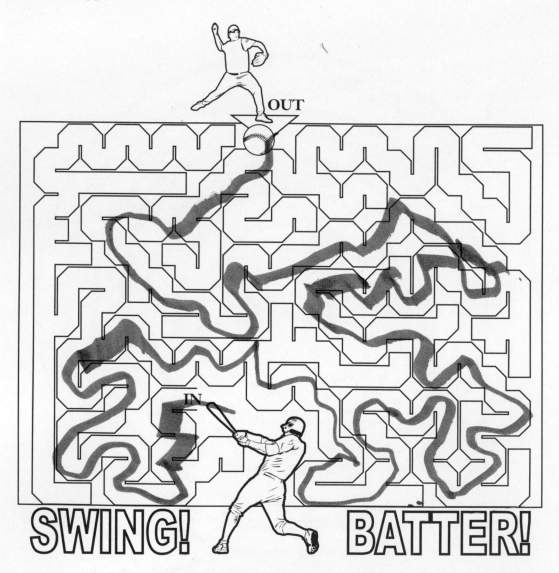

Answer on page 177.

Lightbulb

Can you find your way through the tangled maze? Follow the electric path from points 1, 2, and 3 to turn on the lightbulb at the end to exit. It is okay to retrace your steps.

Answer on page 178.

Volcano

Watch out for molten lava on your way to the volcano.

FINISH

START

Answers on page 178.

Hoops

Make the winning basket to be MVP of the game.

Trivia on the Brain

Basketball was invented in 1891. The very first basket used in the game was a peach basket, not the net we know today.

Answers on page 178.

Boo!

Find your way through this haunted maze—if you dare!

Answers on page 178.

Square Dance

Can you find your way through this sea of squares?

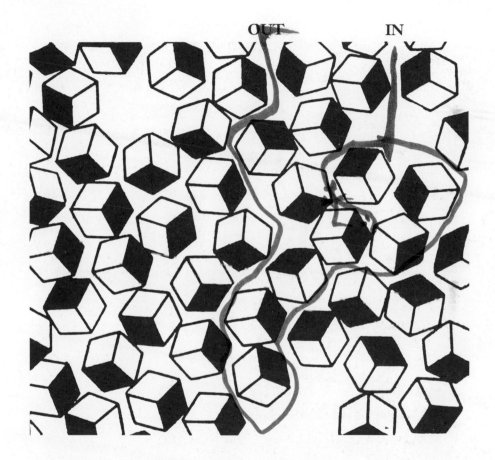

Trivia on the Brain
The square dance is the official dance of 19 states in America including Washington, Illinois, and Tennessee.

Answers on page 178.

Jungle Path

Help this young explorer find his way to the exotic bird stuck in the tree.

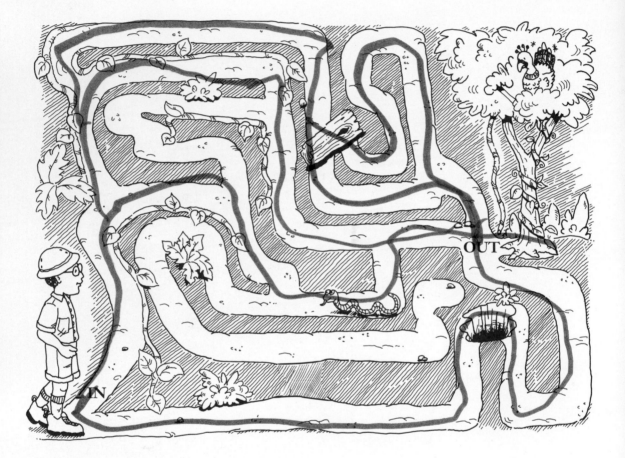

Answer on page 178.

Road Trip!

This confused driver is having trouble finding the gas station—and he's running on empty! Follow the arrows to help him find the correct route.

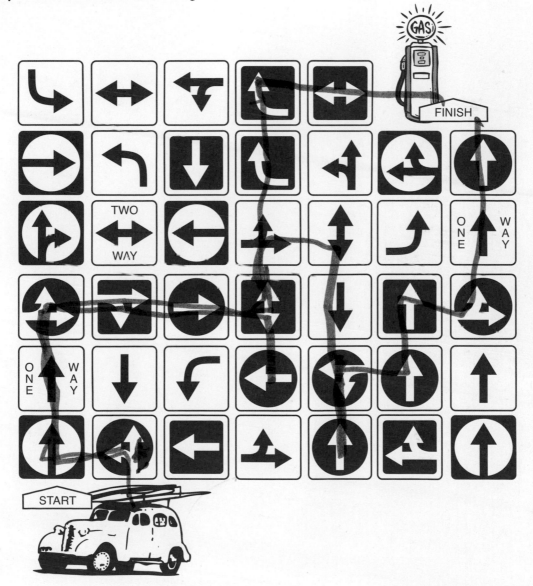

Answer on page 178.

Famished Family

How fast can mom get dinner on the table?

Answer on page 178.

Fishing

Help the fish eat all 5 worms before going home, but be careful—you musn't pass the worms with hooks!

Answer on page 179.

Bee Maze

Help the bee find its way to the flower at the center of the maze.

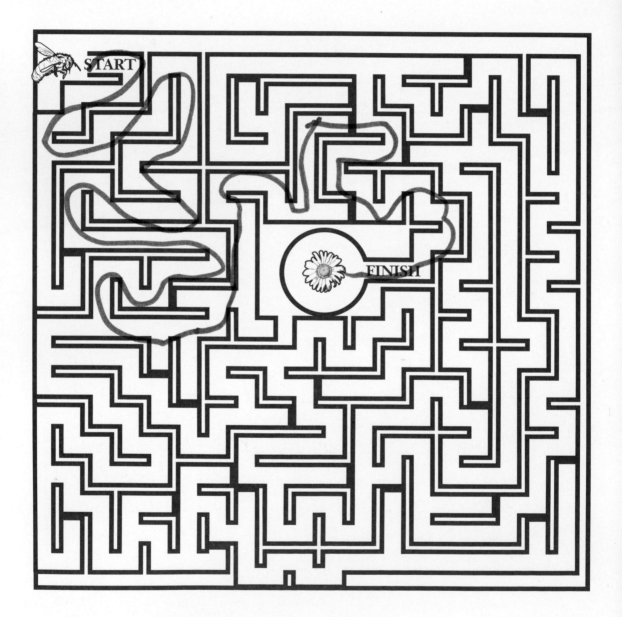

Answer on page 179.

Flower Power

Guide the butterfly to the flower at the end of the maze.

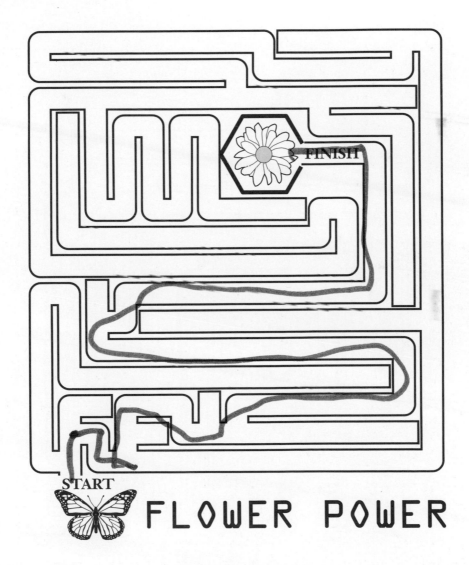

FINISH

START

FLOWER POWER

Answer on page 179.

Feeling Antsy?

These hungry ants have set their sights on your birthday cake!

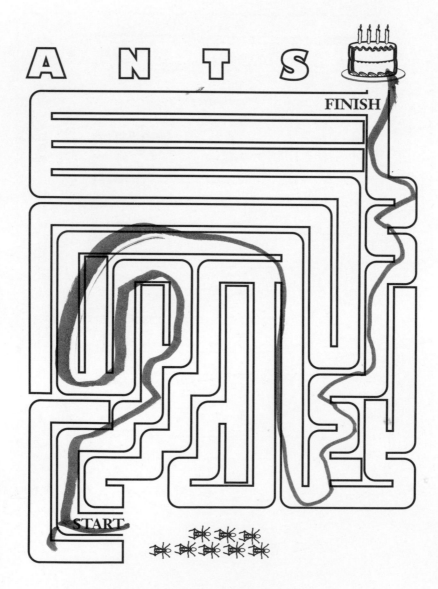

FINISH

START

Answer on page 179.

Home Run!

Follow the slugger's blast to the ball's location in the center of the maze and then out of the park!

Answer on page 179.

75

Treasure Boat

There's only way to get to the treasure at the bottom of this boat—see if you can find it! Use the ladders to move from level to level.

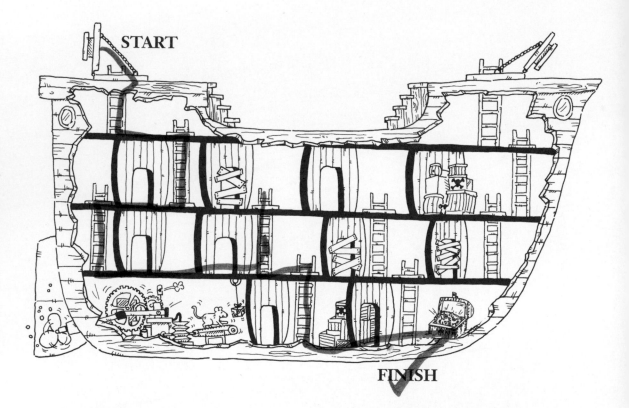

Trivia on the Brain

One of the most famous ships to transport treasure was called *Queen Anne's Revenge* and was captained by the equally famous pirate, Blackbeard. The remains of the ship were found just off the coast of North Carolina in 1996. Do you think Blackbeard lost any treasure down there?

Answer on page 179.

On the Moon

Help this explorer locate the center of the moon where he hopes to find precious metals.

Answer on page 180.

77

Eruption!

You'll have to move pretty quickly to get to the helicopter before the lava does!

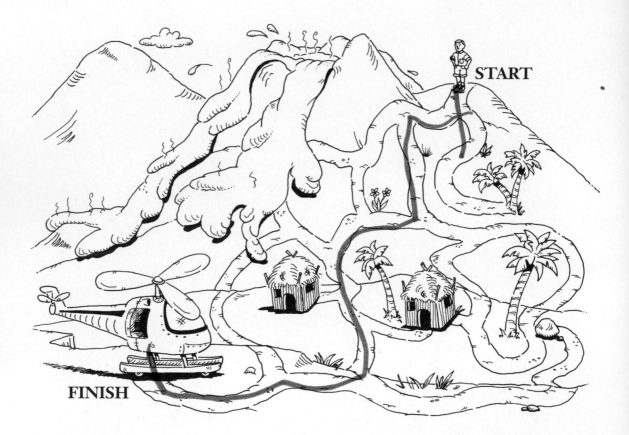

Answer on page 180.

78

Graveyard Shuffle

You're going to have to dig your way out of this maze!

Answer on page 180.

Manic Maze

Can you find your way through the tangled maze?

START

FINISH

Answer on page 180.

Stargazing

Can you find your way through the tangled maze? If so, you're a star!

START

FINISH

Answer on page 180.

81

PICK UP THE PACE

Until the Cow Comes Home

Help the farmer bring this lost cow back to the barn.

Answer on page 180.

Chrome Maze

Congratulations, you've found a maze made of solid chrome! Can you get to the star in the center?

START

FINISH

⚙️ Trivia on the Brain

Many people know chromium is used to make metal (like chrome), but did you know it's used to make colors, too? The most familiar color it can make is one you see almost every day: school-bus (or chrome) yellow!

Answer on page 180.

Rat

This hungry rat is on a quest for cheese. Help him find his way.

Answer on page 181.

Flower Power

Guide the butterfly to the flower at the end of the maze.

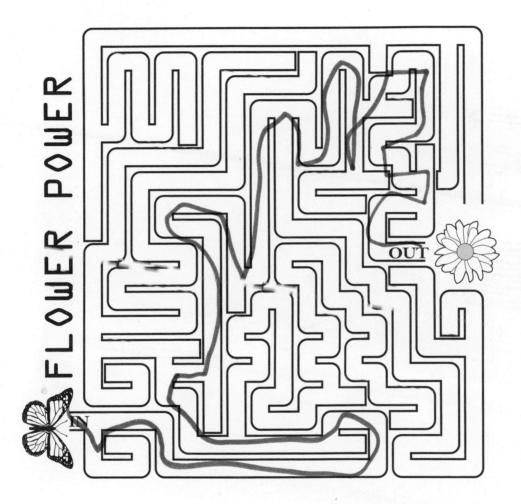

Answer on page 181.

85

Hamster Home

This little hamster can't remember which tunnel leads to his home. Can you help him find the right one? (Note: For this maze, it is okay to cross solid black lines.)

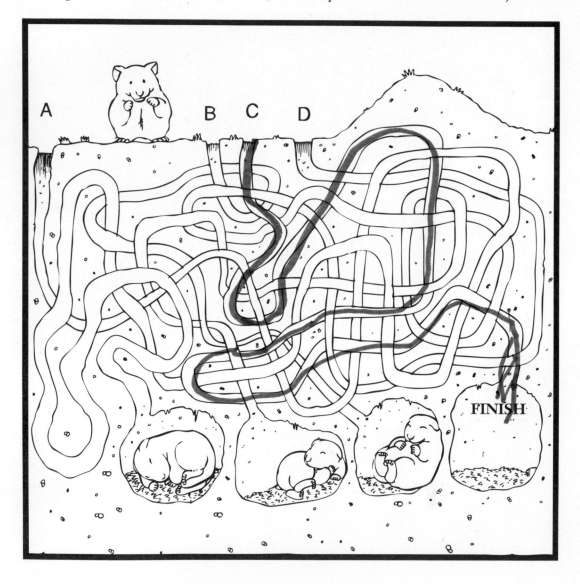

Answer on page 181.

Big Top Maze

Here's your ticket to the circus! Begin at the tent entrance and climb out at the top flag.

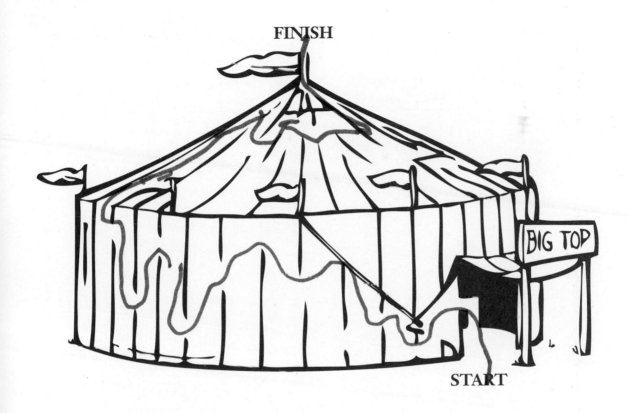

FINISH

START

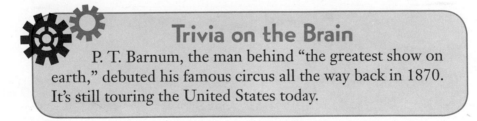

Trivia on the Brain

P. T. Barnum, the man behind "the greatest show on earth," debuted his famous circus all the way back in 1870. It's still touring the United States today.

Answer on page 181.

Honey Bear

Help the bear find a sweet reward at the end of the maze.

Answer on page 181.

Skateboard Sam

Skateboard Sam loves his fruit smoothies, but first he must find his way through the maze.

Answer on page 181.

Cat and Mice

Who will win this game of cat and mouse?

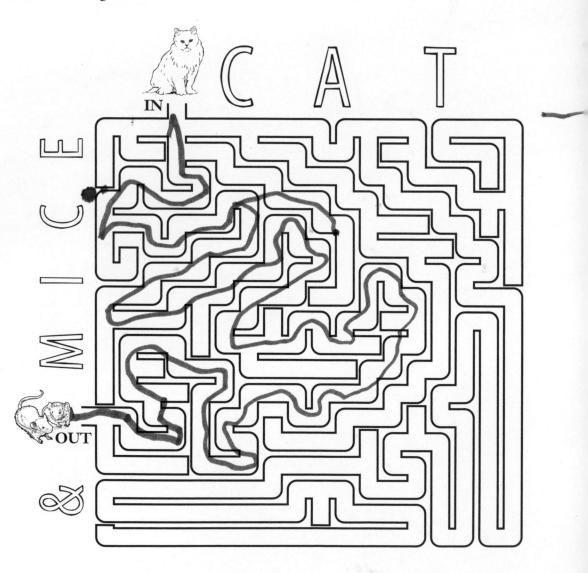

Answer on page 181.

Ants Go Marching

These hungry ants have set their sights on your birthday cake!

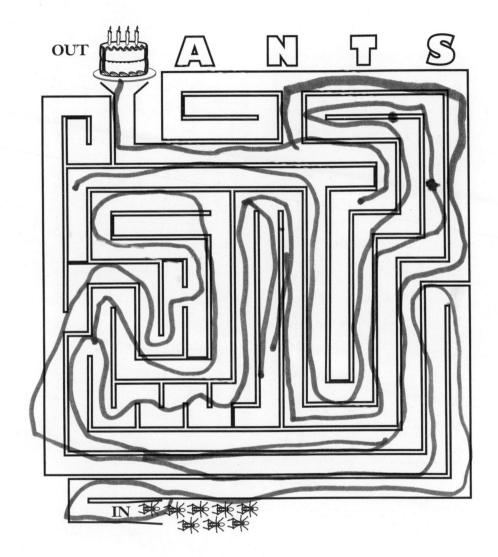

Answer on page 182.

Knot Maze

This maze of hallways seems to be all knotted up. Make your way through the maze without getting tied up.

START

FINISH

Answer on page 182.

92

Yo Ho Ho!

This pirate is on the hunt for buried treasure. Lead him to the treasure chest at the bottom of the maze.

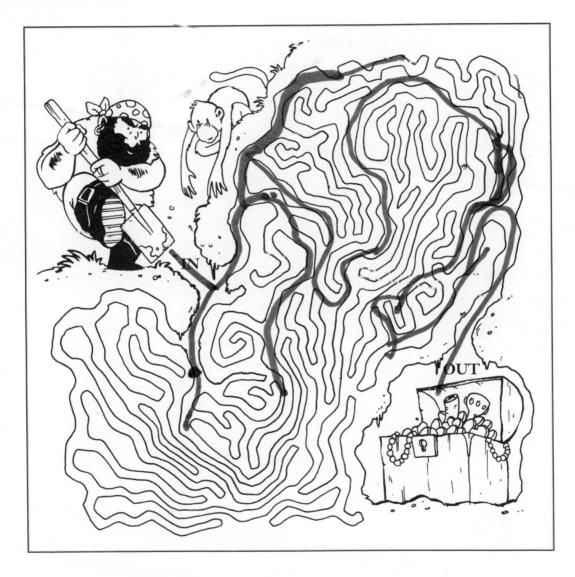

Answer on page 182.

Take a Shot

Make the winning basket to be the MVP of this game.

Trivia on the Brain

Basketball may have been around since the late 1800s, but the NBA wasn't founded until 1946. The first official NBA game was played on November 1, 1946, between the New York Knicks and the Toronto Huskies.

Answer on page 182.

Which Way In?

This circle maze has 5 ways in, but only one entrance leads to the center room.
Which one?

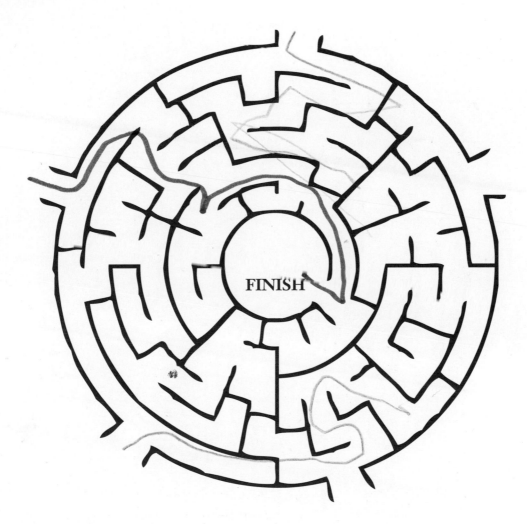

Answer on page 182.

Farmer Maze

Help the farmer bring this lost cow back to the barn.

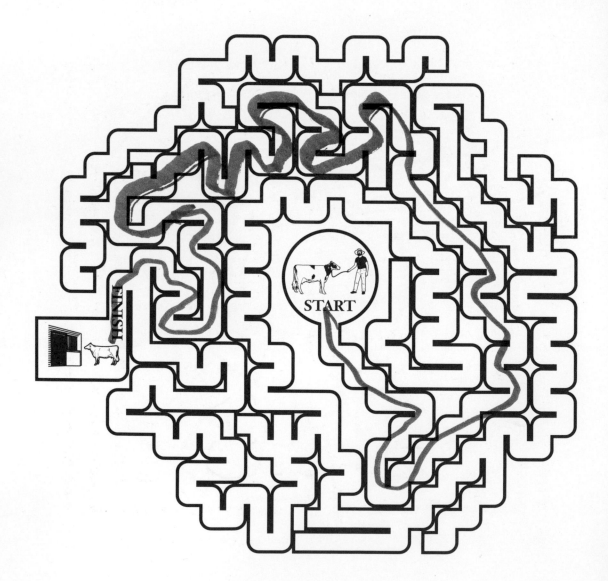

Answer on page 182.

Four-Square Maze

You'd love to see what's inside those 4 center rooms, but they appear to be blocked off. On the other hand, you don't want to get trapped in this strange building! So start at top left and find your way out at bottom right.

START

FINISH

Answer on page 182.

Flower Power

Guide the butterfly to the flower at the end of the maze.

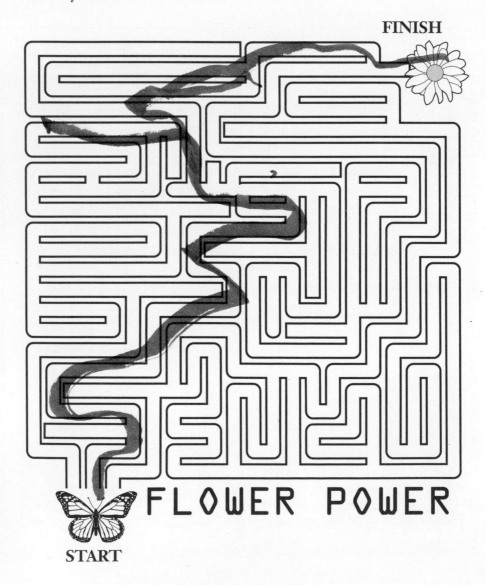

FINISH

START

FLOWER POWER

Answer on page 182.

Breaking the Ice

Lead this penguin back to its egg before it gets too cold.

Answer on page 183.

99

Dog Bone Bakery

Help Billy Bulldog and his pal Mutts find their way through the maze to the Dog Bone Bakery for treats.

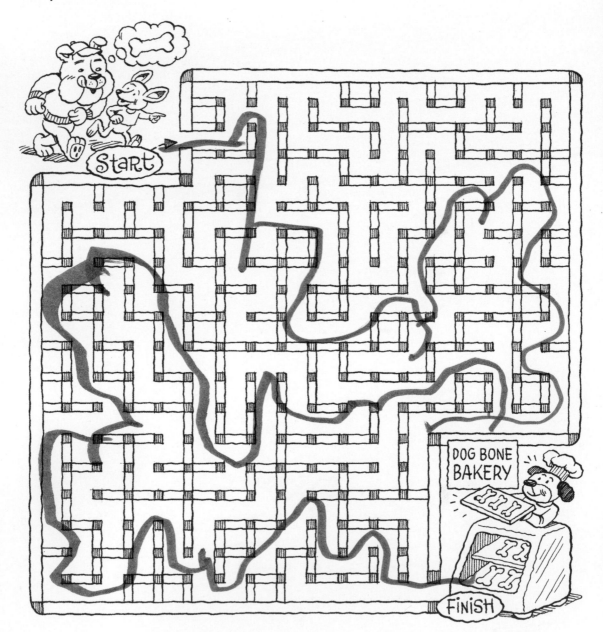

Answer on page 183.

Cruisin'

Choose the path that will lead you to Palm Tree Drive. Only one path will work.

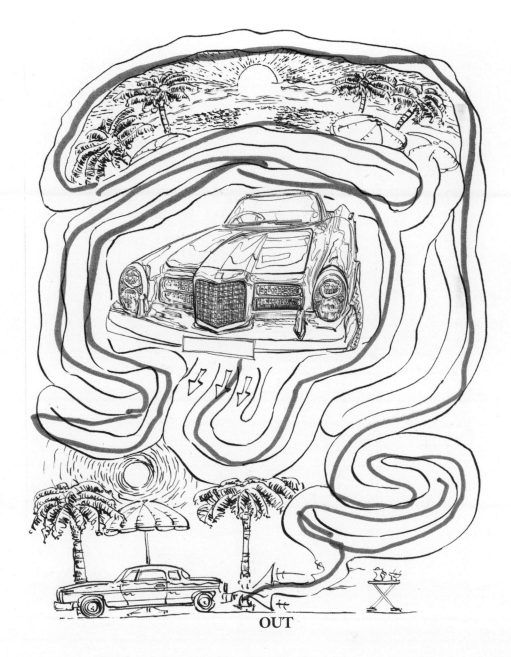

OUT

Answer on page 183.

Honey Bear

Help the bear find a sweet reward at the end of the maze.

HONEY BEAR

Answer on page 183.

Gary's Underground Maze

Gary Groundhog made the tunnel to his burrow too complicated. It's spring, and he needs to find his way out. Maybe you can help.

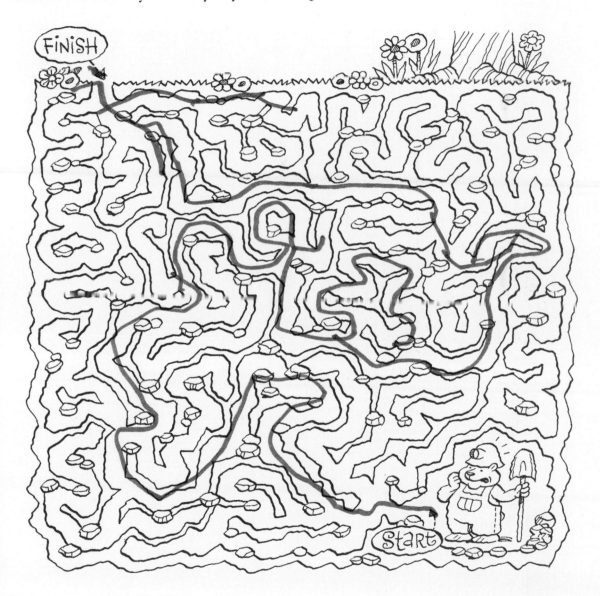

Answer on page 183.

103

Getting There

Should you take a train, boat, or a plane to arrive at your destination? Only one will get you there.

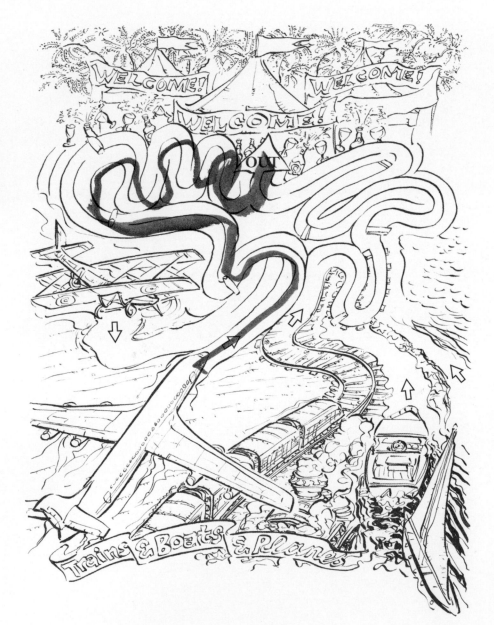

Answer on page 183.

Mind Over Maze

Can you find your way through the tangled maze?

START

FINISH

Answer on page 184.

Turtle Maze

Don't get lost as you navigate your way across the turtle's shell.

START

FINISH

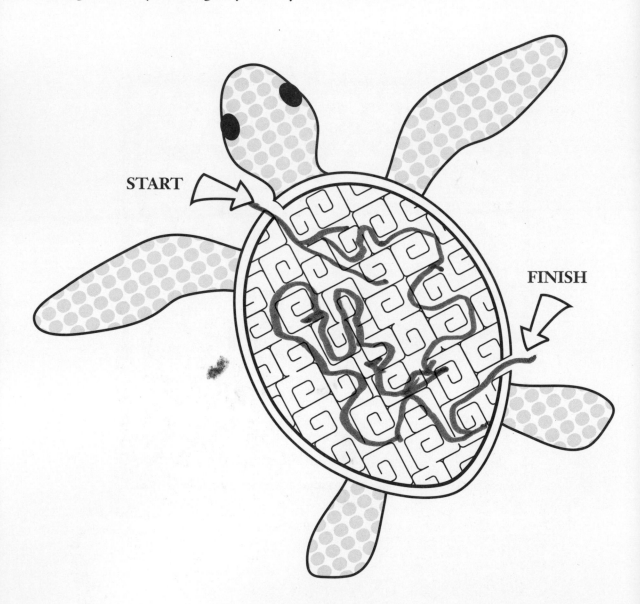

Answer on page 184.

Horsing Around

Seems like this jockey is a little lost. Can you get him to his horse?

Answer on page 184.

107

Lost and Found

Can you find your way through the tangled maze?

START

FINISH

Answer on page 184.

108

Car Chase

These people have had a great day shopping in the city! One problem: They can't find the parking garage to get their car. Can you help?

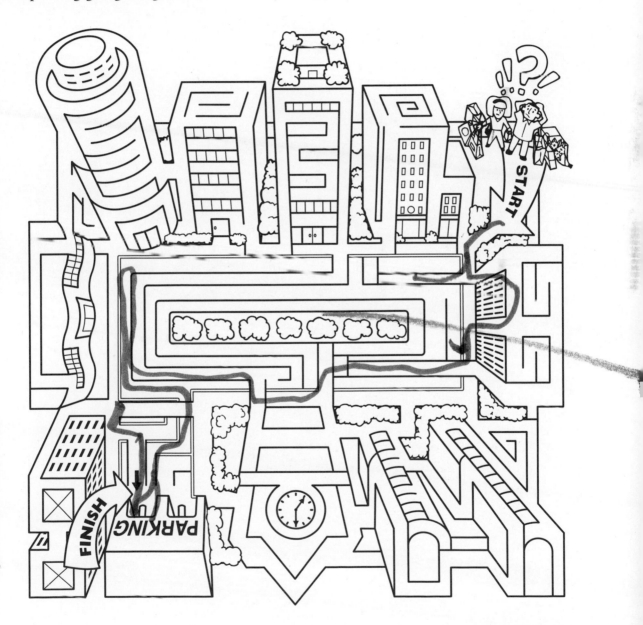

Answer on page 184.

109

Anthill

Help these worker ants get food to their queen. Watch out for the ants blocking the tunnels!

Answer on page 184.

Squared Silly

Can you find your way through the tangled maze?

START

FINISH

Trivia on the Brain

If you're driving through Missouri, you might see one big tangle on the way. Charleston, Missouri, is home to what they're calling the "world's largest hair ball," a 167-pound mass of hair, created by barber Henry Coffer.

Answer on page 184.

Here Kitty!

Uh-oh. Looks like kitty is stuck on the roof of the neighbor's house again. Can you find your way through the haunted rooms to get to the roof? Use the ladders to move from floor to floor.

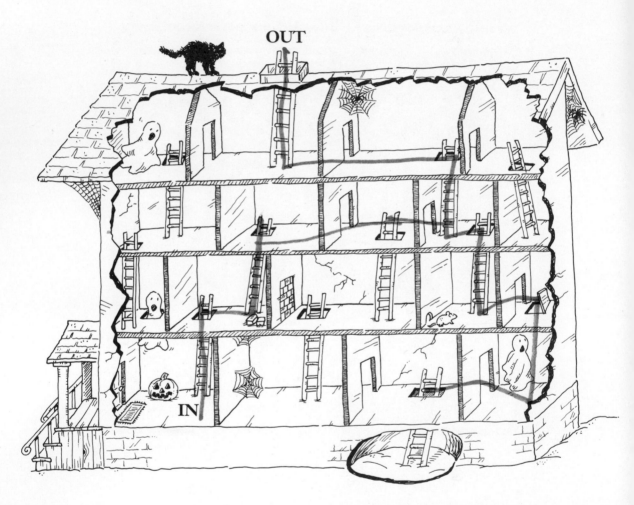

Answers on page 185.

Trotting Along

Start at the arrow and walk your horses down to the gate and back to where you started.

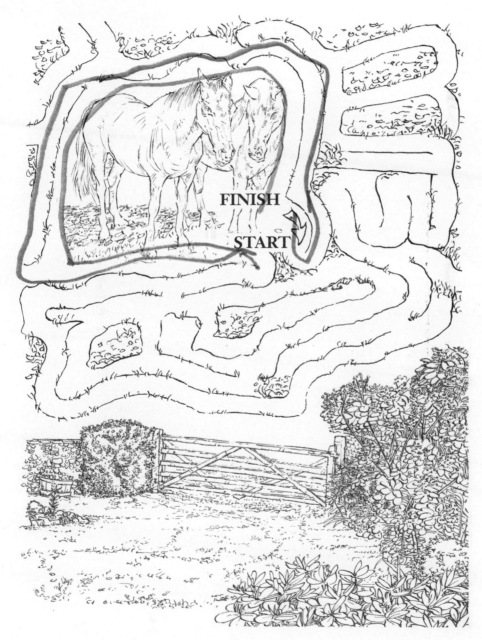

FINISH

START

Answers on page 185.

Shopping Trip

These shoppers want to get home, but a few stops remain. In order—and without retracing your steps—visit the clothes shop, the music shop, the book shop, the shoe shop, and the cafe before finally heading home. Go over and under bridges where necessary.

Answers on page 185.

In or Out?

Can you find your way through the tangled maze?

START

FINISH

Answers on page 185.

115

Crustacean Crossing

Get this crab off the beach and back into the water.

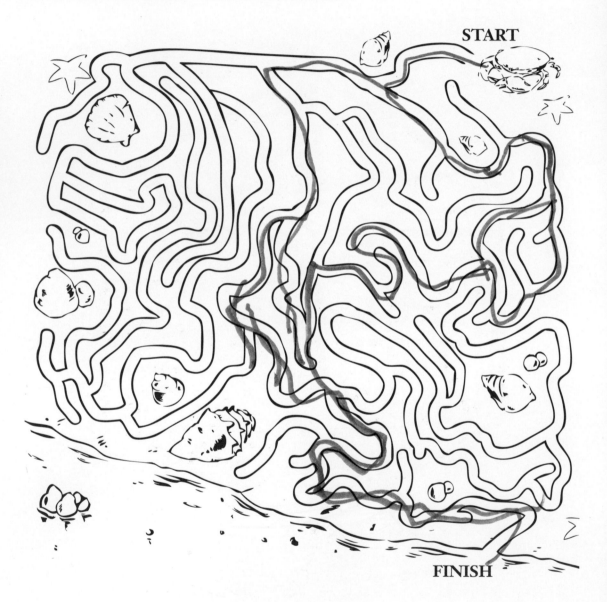

START

FINISH

Answer on page 185.

116

Tornado

Avoid flying debris as you guide this bird through and then out of the tornado.

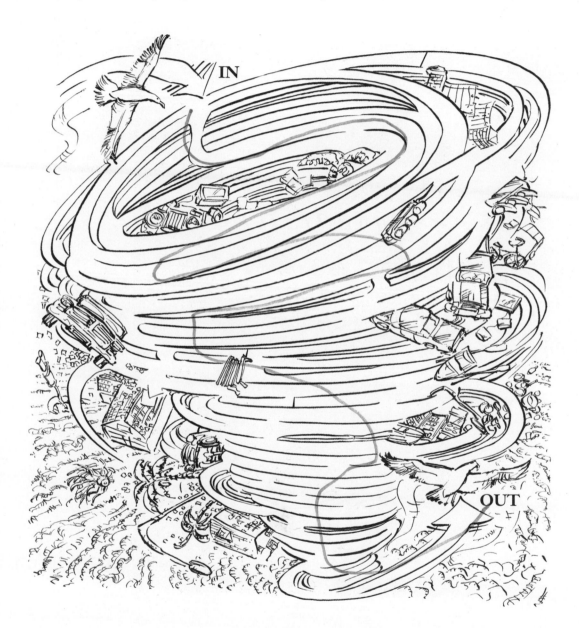

IN

OUT

Answer on page 185.

Get It Straight

Don't get too caught up in all the twists and turns as you negotiate your way to the center of this spiderweb labyrinth.

Answer on page 185.

Road Trip!

This confused driver is having trouble finding the gas station—and he's running on empty! Follow the arrows to help him find the correct route.

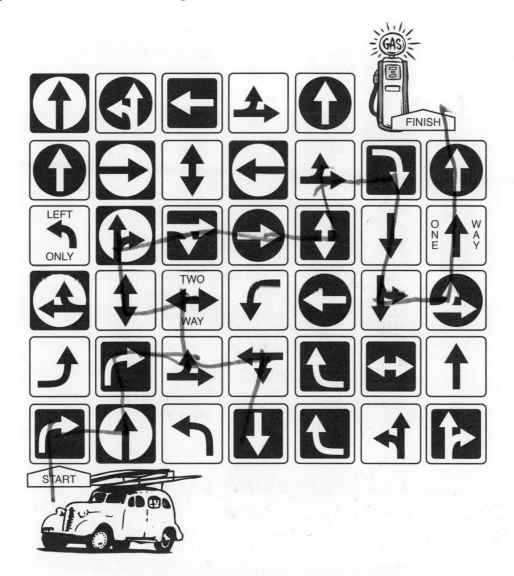

Answer on page 186.

119

In and Out of the House

If you start at the entrance at bottom left, how long will it take you to get out at the right?

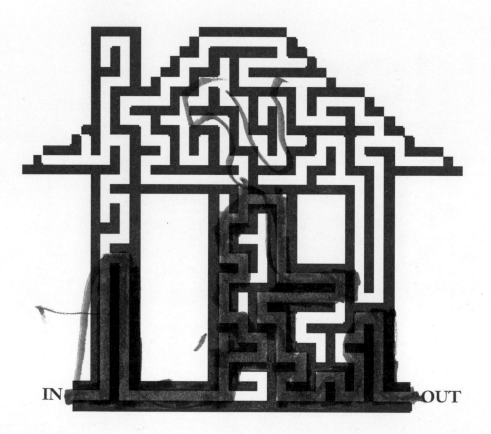

IN · · · · · · · · OUT

⚙⚙ **Trivia on the Brain**

There's a real-life maze of a house in San Jose, California. Its original owner, Sarah Winchester, had the home under constant construction for 38 years, creating a labyrinth complete with doors that lead nowhere, twisting hallways, and dizzying staircases.

Answer on page 186.

Summer Celebration

Enjoy the show as you make your way through the Capitol!

Answer on page 186.

121

Exit Only

Can you find your way through the tangled maze?

START

FINISH

Answer on page 186.

Hoops

Make the winning basket to be MVP of the game.

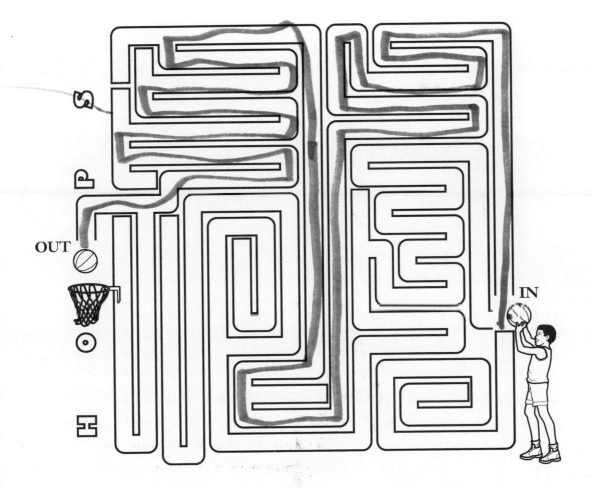

OUT

IN

Answer on page 186.

Home Sweet Home

Watch out for black holes as you help this alien go back to his home planet.

Answer on page 186.

One Way Out

Can you find your way through the tangled maze?

START

FINISH

Answer on page 186.

Honey Bear

Help the bear find a sweet reward at the end of the maze.

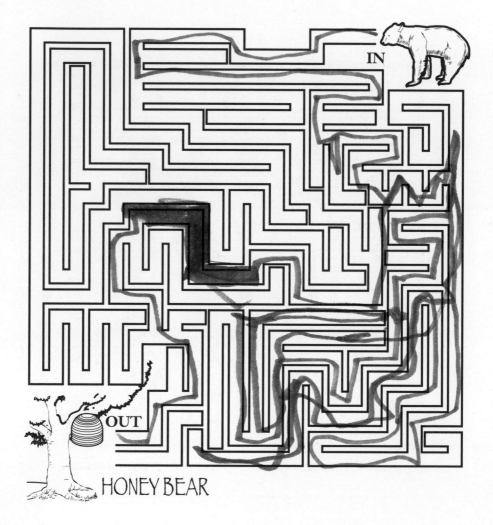

IN

OUT

HONEY BEAR

Answer on page 186.

Cat and Mice

Who will win this game of cat and mouse?

Answer on page 187.

127

Road Trip!

This confused driver is having trouble finding the gas station—and he's running on empty! Follow the arrows to help him find the correct route.

Answer on page 187.

Computer Class

Please help George find his way to room 34 for his computer class.

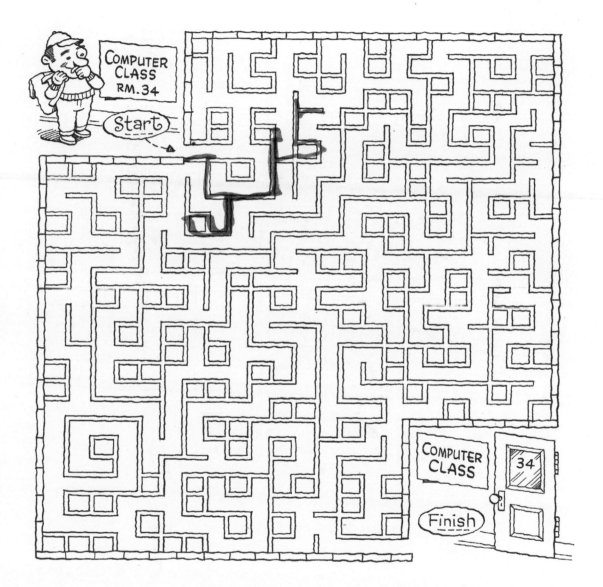

Answer on page 187.

Rescue Mission

This ship's going down! Guide the final crewmember to the exit at the bottom (now the top) of the ship for an aerial rescue.

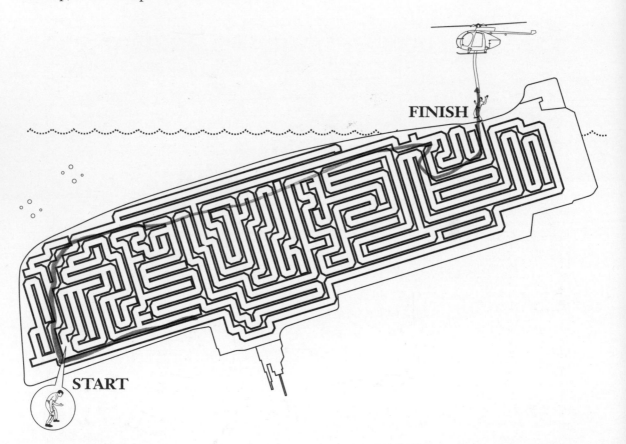

FINISH

START

Answer on page 187.

At the Mall

Help Mary find her way to the food court to meet her friend.

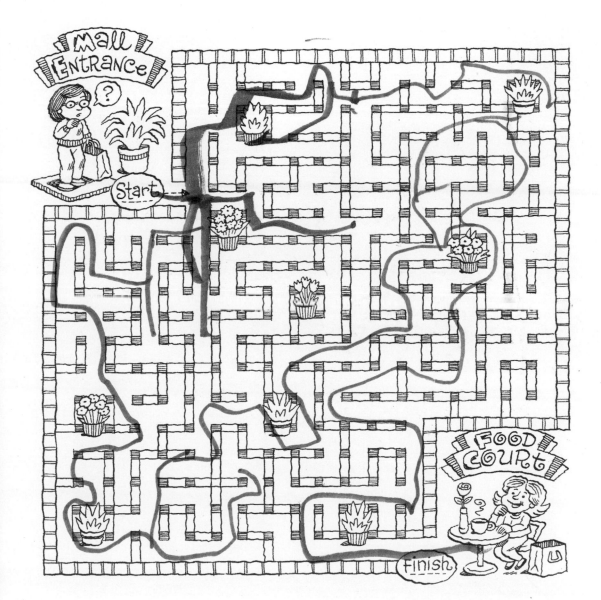

Answer on page 187.

131

Jigsaw Maze

It's hard enough to do a jigsaw puzzle, but now someone has created a maze inside too! Can you put together the correct path?

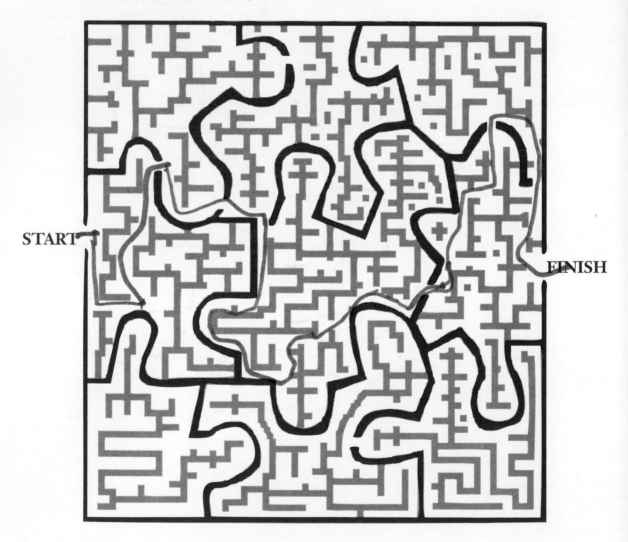

START

FINISH

Answer on page 187.

Road Trip!

This confused driver is having trouble finding the gas station—and he's running on empty! Follow the arrows to help him find the correct route.

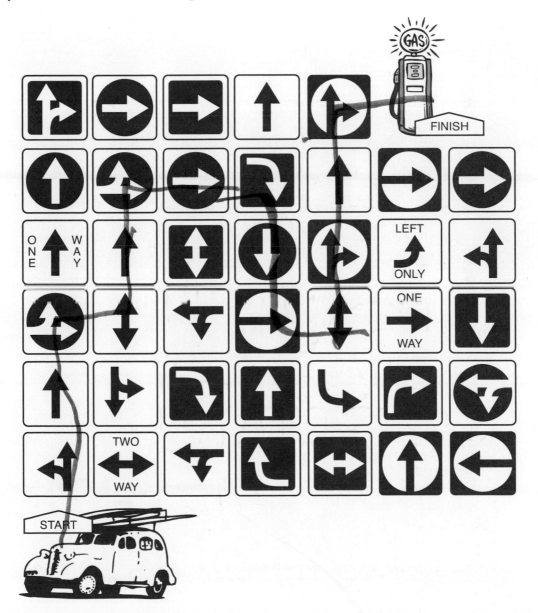

Answer on page 188.

133

Feeling Antsy?

These hungry ants have set their sights on your birthday cake!

OUT

IN ANTS

Answer on page 188.

Twisty Maze

If you've done a lot of mazes by now, you should be ready for this one. It has more twists than a barrel of pretzels! You can travel over and under bridges if necessary.

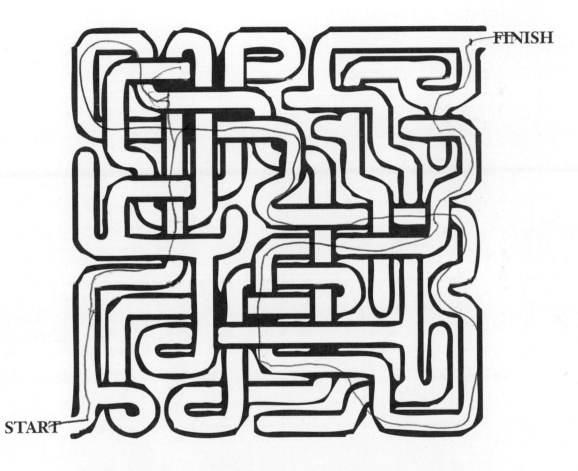

START

FINISH

Trivia on the Brain
Helen Hoff was a champion pretzel twister: She could twist pretzel dough into its familiar shape at a rate of 57 pretzels a minute!

Answer on page 188.

Apple Maze

Start at the center of the apple, and help the worm chew his way out!

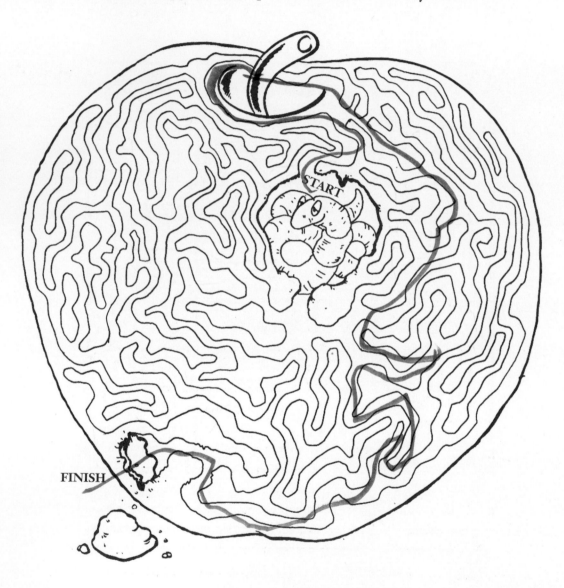

START

FINISH

Answer on page 188.

Cat and Mice

Who will win this game of cat and mouse?

Answer on page 188.

137

Space Race

Help these aliens find their way to their home planet.

Answer on page 188.

138

Pete's Pizza Delivery

Please help Pete find the shortest route through the maze to deliver pizzas to his favorite customers, the O'Hares.

Answer on page 188.

Firebreather!

Find your way through this fun dragon maze.

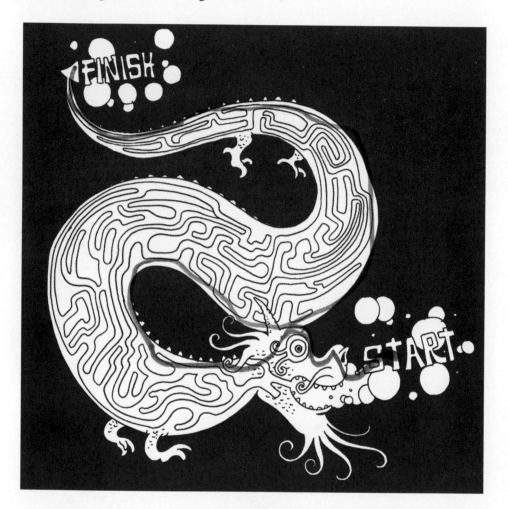

Trivia on the Brain

Dragons might seem scary to us, but in Chinese culture, dragons are symbols of power and strength. They're even thought to be good luck.

Answer on page 188.

Around the Next Bend

Find your way through the tangled maze.

Answer on page 189.

Larry's Lawnmower

Larry has cut a maze into his yard, but now he must find his way through it to put away his mower. Can you help him?

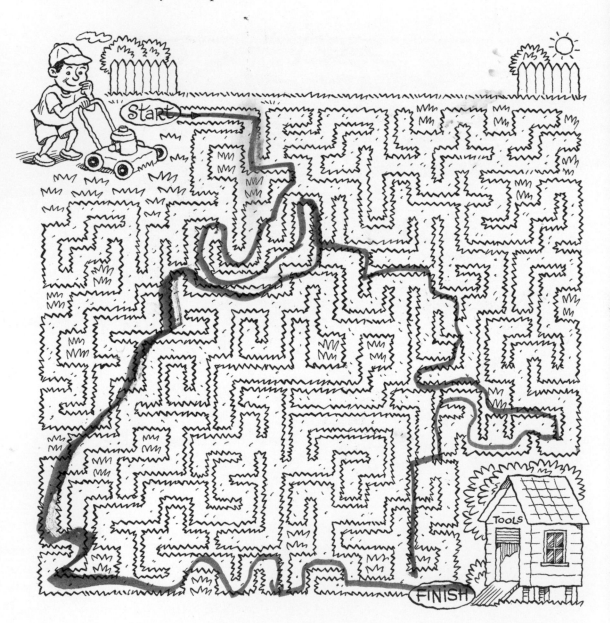

Answer on page 189.

Triangle Trouble

Find your way through the tangled maze.

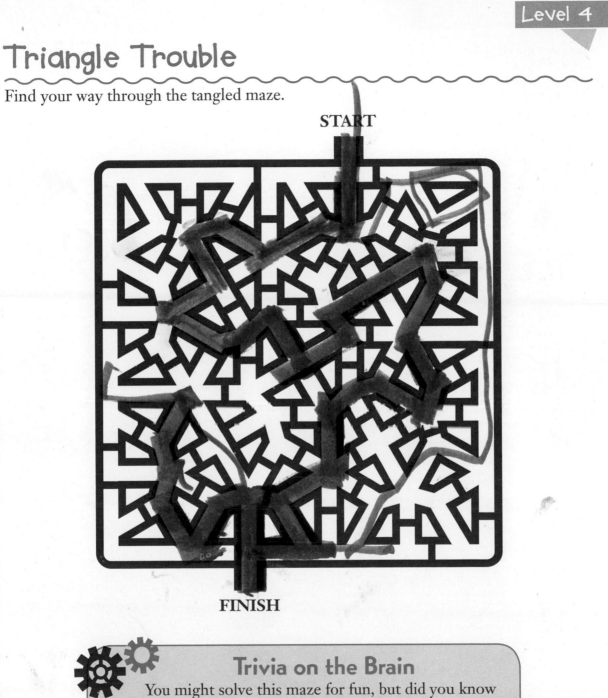

Trivia on the Brain

You might solve this maze for fun, but did you know mazes are used in psychological experiments? Psychologists use mazes to study spatial navigation and learning and often employ rats and mice to run through the mazes.

Answer on page 189.

Mountain Climber

Henry wants to hike to the mountain's summit, and he needs your help to find the right path.

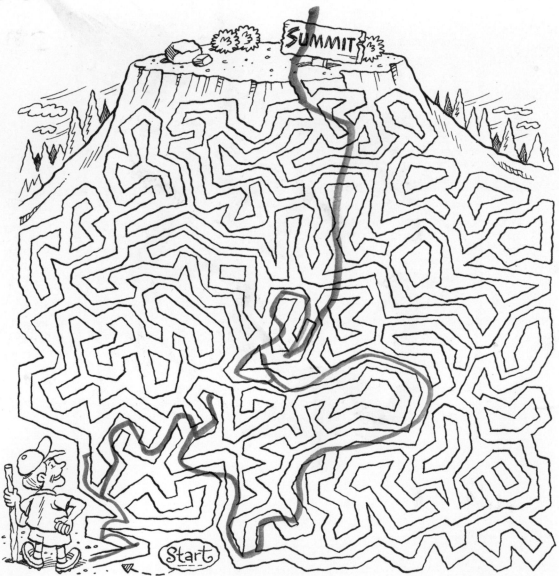

Answer on page 189.

Get It Straight

Don't get too caught up in all the twists and turns as you negotiate your way to the center of this intricate sheep labyrinth.

Trivia on the Brain

Sheep have a special place in the field of science; in 1995 a sheep named Dolly was the first mammal cloned from an adult sheep's cell.

Answer on page 189.

Honey Bear

Help this hungry bear find his way to the honeycomb.

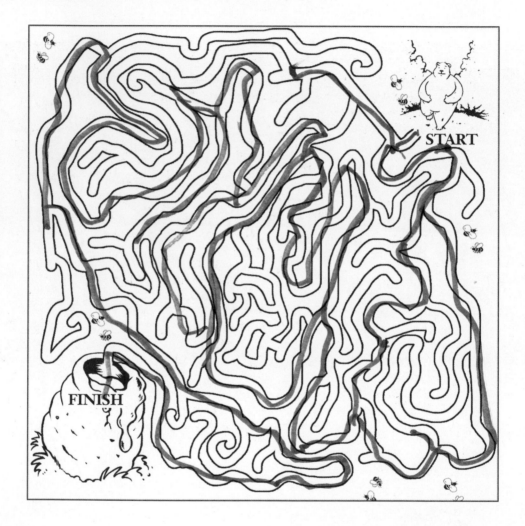

Answer on page 189.

Walking Trail

This hiker is tired and lost. Help him get back to his campsite.

Answer on page 189.

Home Run!

Follow the slugger's blast to hit the ball out of the park

Answer on page 189.

148

At a Snail's Pace

Don't get too caught up in the twists and turns of this snail maze!

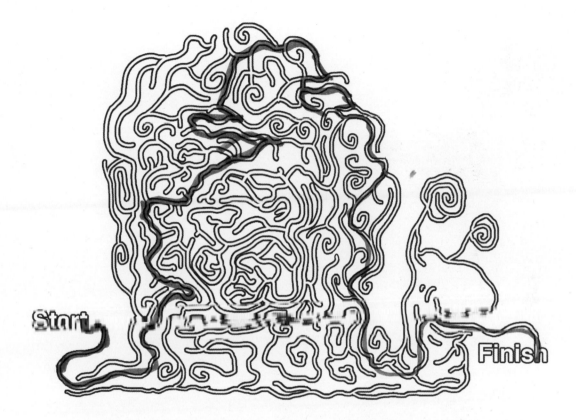

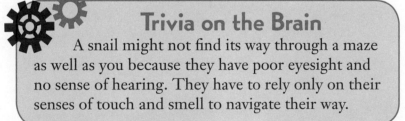

Trivia on the Brain

A snail might not find its way through a maze as well as you because they have poor eyesight and no sense of hearing. They have to rely only on their senses of touch and smell to navigate their way.

Answer on page 190.

Ferret Your Way Out

This ferret made a mess! Find your way through the tubing to reconnect the wires. You can travel over and under bridges if necessary.

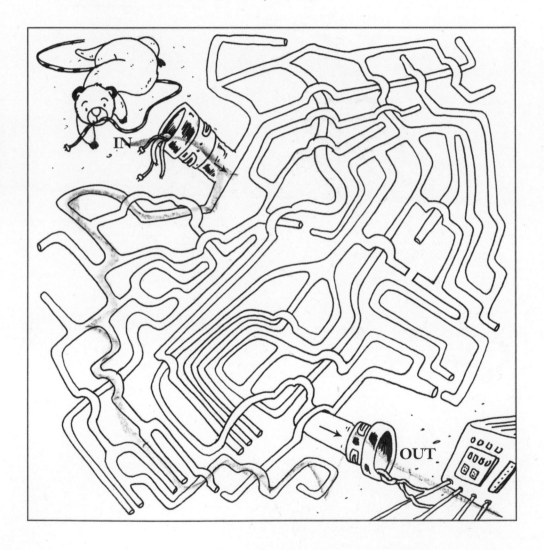

Answer on page 190.

Cake Mix

Help the baker collect all of his ingredients (by passing through their circles) on his way through this maze.

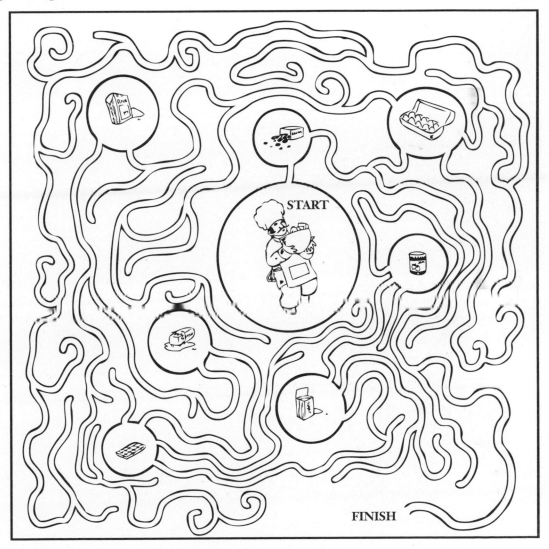

Answer on page 190.

Art Smarts

This maze is a work of art! Make your way from start to finish.

Answer on page 190.

A Pixie Picnic

Help the pixies get to the picnic.

Answer on page 190.

Treasure Castle

The knight must choose the right path from start to finish that will help him avoid the dragon and lead him to riches.

Answer on page 190.

154

Stuck

This camper is stuck in a swamp. Help him get to dry land.

Answer on page 190.

Recycling Pathway

Can you help each child deliver their recyclables to the correct bin?

Answer on page 190.

A Snarled Web

Can you find your way through the tangled maze?

Answer on page 191.

Feeling Antsy?

These hungry ants have set their sights on your birthday cake!

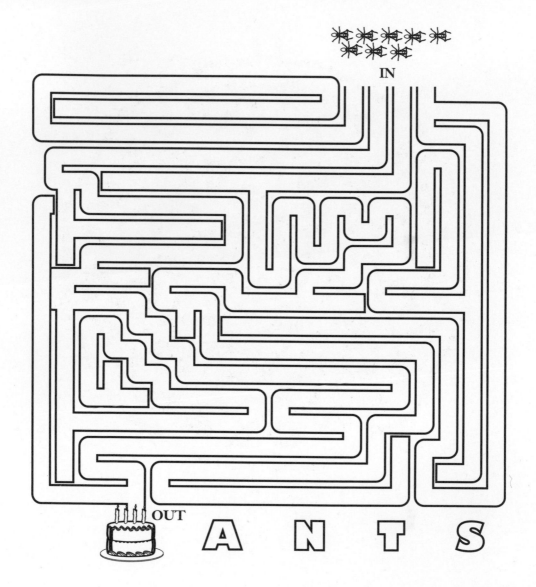

IN

OUT

A N T S

Answer on page 191.

Penguin Pals Maze

Perry Penguin might need some help joining his pal for ice hockey. Find the way through from start to finish.

Answer on page 191.

Waterslide

Help Jimmy find the chute that will lead him to the pool below. Jimmy can travel over and under bridges if necessary.

Answer on page 191.

Road Trip!

This confused driver is having trouble finding the gas station—and he's running on empty! Follow the arrows to help him find the correct route.

Answer on page 191.

Sally's Shopping Trip

Sally must shop for milk, eggs, and bread in that order as she finds her way through the maze to the check-out.

Answer on page 191.

162

Lizard Hijinks

Help the lizard finds its way through the garden hose. He can travel over and under bridges if necessary.

IN

OUT

Answer on page 192.

Cat and Mice

Who will win this game of cat and mouse?

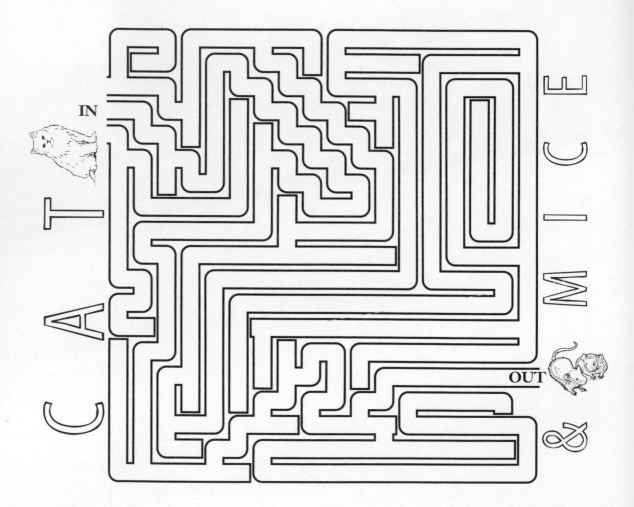

Answer on page 192.

Sarah's Desert

Help Sarah and Sugarfoot find their way through the desert to Cactus Creek.

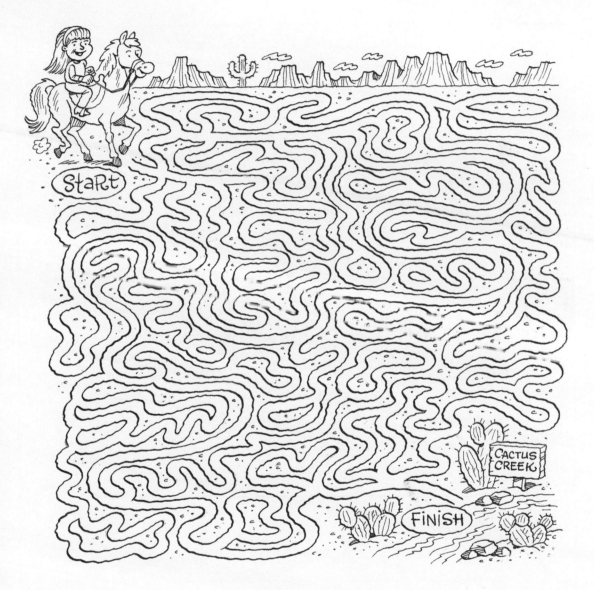

Answer on page 192.

165

Follow the Trail

Follow the correct trail to get to the top of the mountain. Travel over and under bridges if necessary.

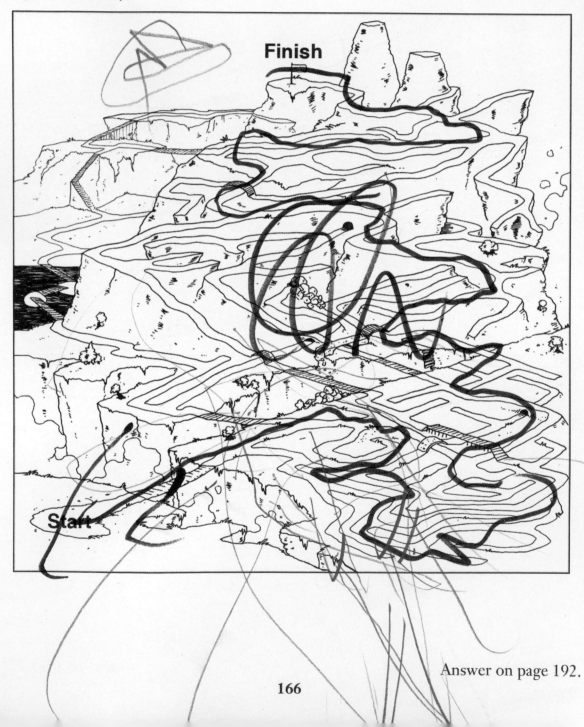

Answer on page 192.

Pigs at the Beach

Help Pete and his pal find their way through the maze to meet their friend at the beach.

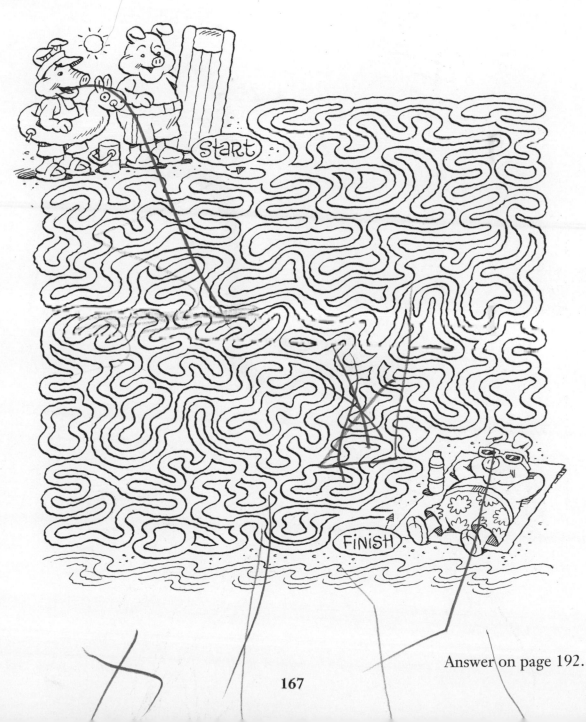

Answer on page 192.

167

Guitar Hero

Which guitar will lead to the amp below? Find out if you want to be a rock star!

Answer on page 192.

ANSWERS

Dino-Mite Maze (page 6)

X Marks the Spot! (page 9)

Tangled Triangles (page 7)

Lost in Space (page 10)

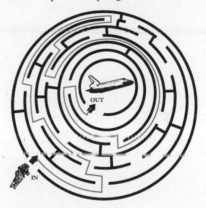

Alley Cat (page 8)

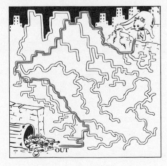

Timer Maze (page 11)

169

Answers

Hoops (page 12)

Monster Mash (page 13)

Feeling Antsy? (page 14)

Box Maze (page 15)

Flower Power (page 16)

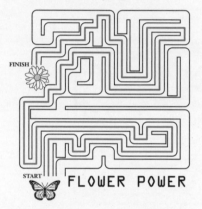

Gone Fishin' (page 17)

What's Cookin'? (page 18)

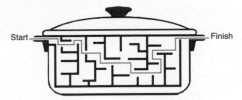

Swing Batter! (page 19)

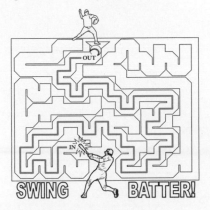

Bee Maze (page 20)

Scrambled Squares (page 21)

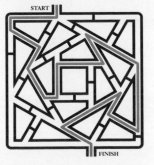

Leapfrog (page 22)

It's the Great Pumpkin Maze! (page 23)

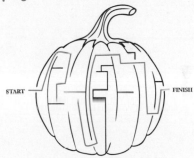

Garden Path (page 24)

Answers

So You Want to Be a Star? (page 25)

Tentacles! (page 28)

Pizza Pie (page 26)

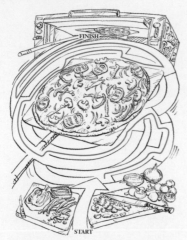

David and Goliath (page 29)

Twist and Shout (page 27)

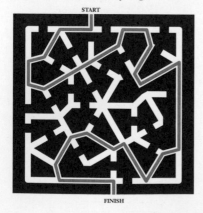

Frosty the Snow-Maze (page 30)

Dizzy Maze (page 31)

Answers

Get It Straight (page 32)

Knotted Network (page 33)

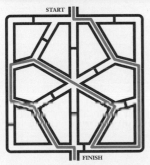

Cottage Stroll (page 34)

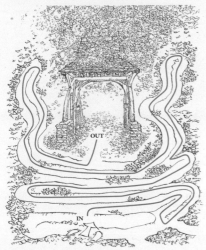

Home Run! (page 35)

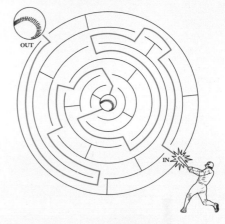

Pizza Delivery! (page 36)

Nell (page 37)

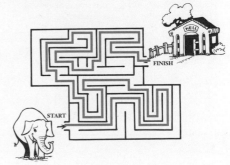

Answers

Cat and Mice (page 38)

A-Maze-ing Walk in the Park (page 39)

Honey Bear (page 40)

Robot Recharge (page 41)

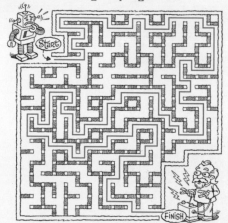

Kittens (page 42)

Granny Smith (page 43)

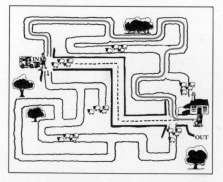

A Whale of a Maze (page 44)

Alien Invasion! (page 45)

Crumbs (page 46)

Nuts and Bolts (page 47)

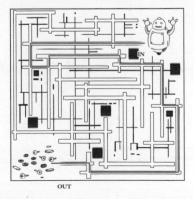

Caveman (page 48)

Here, Fishy Fishy! (page 49)

Busy Bees (page 50)

Answers

Pondemonium (page 51)

Yer Out! (page 52)

Warp Drive! (page 53)

Snack Attack (page 54)

Here Kitty! (page 55)

Cafeteria Confusion (page 56)

Trapped! (page 57)

Garden (page 58)

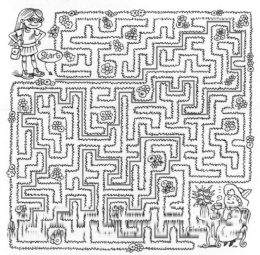

Game Time! (page 59)

Wild Wally's Waterpark (page 60)

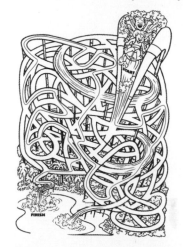

Out of this World! (page 61)

Batter Up! (page 62)

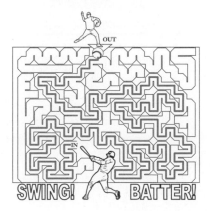

Answers

Lightbulb (page 63)

Square Dance (page 67)

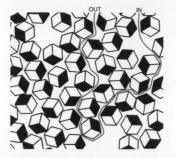

Volcano (page 64)

Jungle Path (page 68)

Hoops (page 65)

Road Trip! (page 69)

Boo! (page 66)

Famished Family (page 70)

Fishing (page 71)

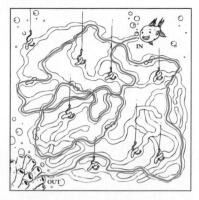

Bee Maze (page 72)

Flower Power (page 73)

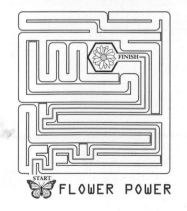

Feeling Antsy? (page 74)

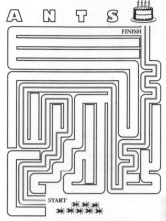

Home Run! (page 75)

Treasure Boat (page 76)

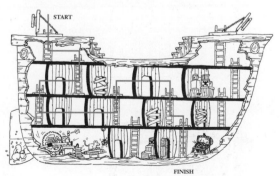

Answers

On the Moon (page 77)

Eruption! (page 78)

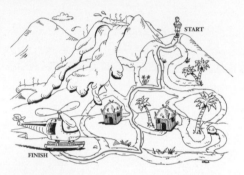

Graveyard Shuffle (page 79)

Manic Maze (page 80)

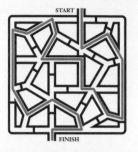

Stargazing (page 81)

Until the Cow Comes Home (page 82)

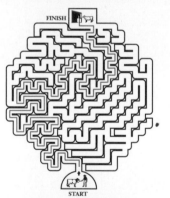

Chrome Maze (page 83)

Answers

Rat (page 84)

Flower Power (page 85)

Hamster Home (page 86)

The correct tunnel to G.

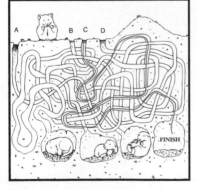

Big Top Maze (page 87)

Honey Bear (page 88)

Skateboard Sam (page 89)

Cat and Mice (page 90)

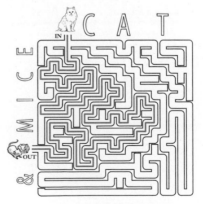

181

Answers

Ants Go Marching (page 91)

Knot Maze (page 92)

Yo Ho Ho! (page 93)

Take a Shot (page 94)

Which Way In? (page 95)

Farmer Maze (page 96)

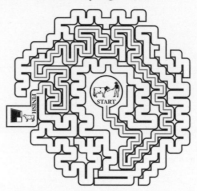

Four-Square Maze (page 97)

Flower Power (page 98)

Breaking the Ice (page 99)

Honey Bear (page 102)

Dog Bone Bakery (page 100)

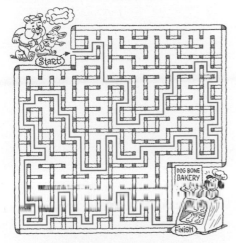

Gary's Underground Maze (page 103)

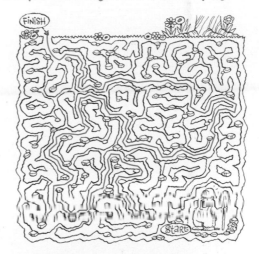

Cruisin' (page 101)

Getting There (page 104)

Answers

Mind Over Maze (page 105)

Lost and Found (page 108)

Turtle Maze (page 106)

Car Chase (page 109)

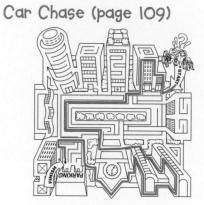

Horsing Around (page 107)

Anthill (page 110)

Squared Silly (page 111)

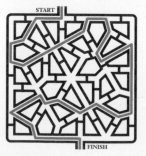

Here Kitty! (page 112)

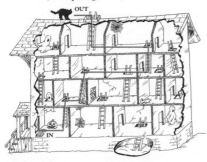

Crustacean Crossing (page 116)

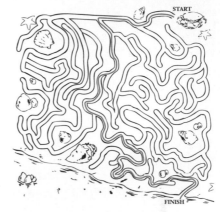

Trotting Along (page 113)

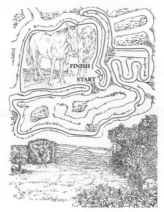

Tornado (page 117)

Chopping Trip (page 114)

Get It Straight (page 118)

In or Out? (page 115)

Answers

Road Trip! (page 119)

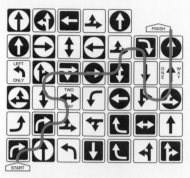

In and Out of the House (page 120)

Summer Celebration (page 121)

Exit Only (page 122)

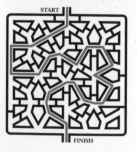

Hoops (page 123)

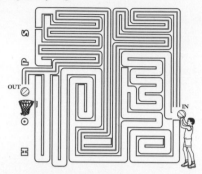

Home Sweet Home (page 124)

One Way Out (page 125)

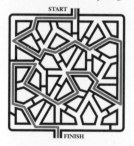

Honey Bear (page 126)

Answers

Cat and Mice (page 127)

Road Trip! (page 128)

Computer Class (page 129)

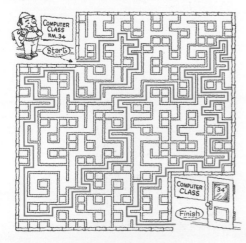

Rescue Mission (page 130)

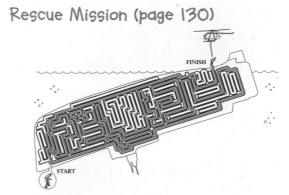

At the Mall (page 131)

Jigsaw Maze (page 132)

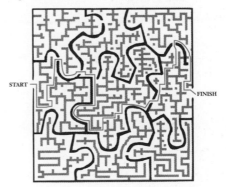

187

Answers

Road Trip! (page 133)

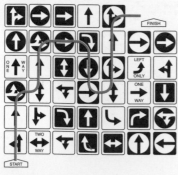

Cat and Mice (page 137)

Feeling Antsy? (page 134)

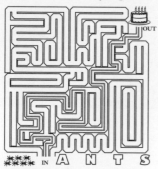

Space Race (page 138)

Twisty Maze (page 135)

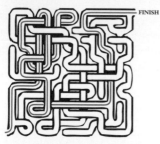

Pete's Pizza Delivery (page 139)

Apple Maze (page 136)

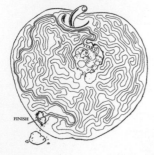

Firebreather! (page 140)

Answers

Around the Next Bend (page 141)

Larry's Lawnmower (page 142)

Triangle Trouble (page 143)

Mountain Climber (page 144)

Get It Straight (page 145)

Honey Bear (page 146)

Walking Trail (page 147)

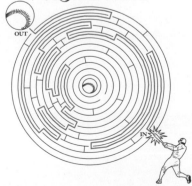

Home Run! (page 148)

Answers

At a Snail's Pace (page 149)

Ferret Your Way Out (page 150)

Cake Mix (page 151)

Art Smarts (page 152)

A Pixie Picnic (page 153)

Treasure Castle (page 154)

Stuck (page 155)

Recycling Pathway (page 156)

Answers

A Snarled Web (page 157)

Feeling Antsy? (page 158)

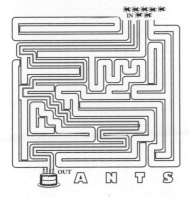

Penguin Pals Maze (page 159)

Waterslide (page 160)

Road Trip! (page 161)

Sally's Shopping Trip (page 162)

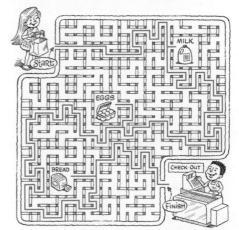

Answers

Lizard Hijinxs (page 163)

Cat and Mice (page 164)

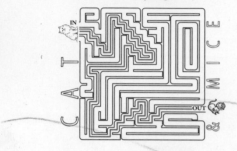

Sarah's Desert (page 165)

Follow the Trail (page 166)

Pigs at the Beach (page 167)

Guitar Hero (page 168)